Wayward Brother

A Gideon Johann Western Book 8

By
Duane Boehm

Wayward Brother: A Gideon Johann Western Book 8

For more information or permission contact:
boehmduane@gmail.com

ISBN: 978-17-90608-29-4

Other Books by Duane Boehm

In Just One Moment
Gideon Johann: A Gideon Johann Western Prequel
Last Stand: A Gideon Johann Western Book 1
Last Chance: A Gideon Johann Western Book 2
Last Hope: A Gideon Johann Western Book 3
Last Ride: A Gideon Johann Western Book 4
Last Breath: A Gideon Johann Western Book 5
Last Journey: A Gideon Johann Western Book 6
Last Atonement: A Gideon Johann Western Book 7
Where The Wild Horses Roam: Wild Horse Westerns Book 1
Spirit Of The Wild Horse: Wild Horse Westerns Book 2
Wild Horse On The Run: Wild Horse Westerns Book 3
What It All Comes Down To
Hand Of Fate: The Hand Of Westerns Book 1
Hand Of The Father: The Hand Of Westerns Book 2
Trail To Yesterday
Sun Over The Mountains
Wanted: A Collection of Western Stories (7 authors)
Wanted II: A Collection of Western Stories (7 authors)

In memory of Uncle Donald – we gave those quail and pheasant hell

Chapter 1

Deputy Finnie Ford strolled into the jail and lowered his short, stout frame into a seat in front of Sheriff Gideon Johann's desk. His arrival didn't even prompt Gideon to look up from the papers scattered in front of him. Finnie had watched the sheriff's mood sink all day long after Gideon had opened a fresh batch of wanted posters that morning. In them, he had found a poster for Fred Parsons after his escape from the Colorado State Penitentiary. Fred had fought alongside Gideon and Finnie in the War Between the States before turning to a life of crime.

As Finnie dropped his hat onto the floor, he asked in his heavy Irish brogue, "All right, why is Fred's escape bothering you so much?"

Gideon glanced up, annoyed he was such an easy read for his friend. Out of habit, he rubbed the scar on his cheekbone as he thought about the question. "Lots of reasons, I guess, Finnie. He was one of us. We three all looked out for each other. I doubt any of us would be alive without the other two. I know for a fact I'd have been dead that time my horse threw me, and that Reb was charging down on me until Fred shot him out of the saddle. For God's sake, how did Fred end up deciding to be an outlaw? I would have trusted him with my last cent."

"Fred was as good a soldier as there was when it came to fighting, but he always was a little on the lazy side as far as camp duty went. I think most outlaws take up crime because they're too sorry to make an honest living."

"That may well be, but what if he comes through here headed home to Pagosa Springs?"

"You're the one that put him in prison. Why are you worried about him showing up in Last Stand?"

"I didn't know it was going to be Fred when we caught him, and I had the sheriff from Silverton there, so I didn't have to think about what I would have done if I'd been on my own. I don't know that I could make myself bring him in if he shows up here," Gideon said as he leaned back in his chair and ran a hand through his long, unruly hair.

"You're getting yourself all worked up over probably nothing. I doubt Fred would show up around Last Stand knowing you're the sheriff. I guess he doesn't even know I'm here. He probably still thinks I'm the town drunk in Animas City. No matter what, you'll do what's right if it comes to it."

"I don't know, Finnie. I just don't know."

Before the conversation could go any further, Doc Abram ambled slowly into the office. His grandson, Henry Hamilton, walked in behind him. The young man hailed from Boston and had just completed his first year at Harvard hoping to follow his grandfather into the medical profession. He was spending the summer with Doc to learn all he could from the practiced physician.

The old doctor had started using a cane the previous year as he recovered after being shot by saloon owner, Cyrus Capello. His friends had noticed that Doc no longer used the cane to bear weight but seemed to have developed a fondness for having it with him, nonetheless. The cane was a source of irritation to everyone else, though, as the doctor was in the habit of leaning it against his chair as he sat down, from where it would invariably fall to the floor, making a racket. To top things off, Doc had recently replaced the cane with a walking stick with a heavy brass knob that made even more noise when it clattered to the floor.

Doc dropped into a chair beside Finnie and leaned his walking stick against it. "I just had to sew up the hand of one of those prospectors. The darn fool paid me in gold dust. I asked him if I looked like I ran a mercantile," he groused.

Finnie turned his head and gave the doctor a hard look. "You should just be glad you got paid. I wouldn't complain if somebody paid me in gold. As a boy, I worked for a potato and was mighty glad to get it."

Throwing his hands in the air, Doc said, "Gideon, have you ever known an Irishman that didn't work a potato into his life story. I'm surprised a spud isn't their national symbol." When the doctor dropped his arms, he knocked the cane to the floor.

Once Finnie had scooped up the walking stick, he shook it at Doc and said, "You're going to knock a hole in our floor with your dandy stick."

Gideon started rubbing his scar again. He'd heard Doc and Finnie fuss at each other a million times it seemed, and he wasn't in the mood for it today. "All right, you two, enough. I think we can all agree that the miners have been a burden to us all."

In the last year, a prospector had made a small find of gold in a creek near the town. Word had spread like wildfire, and soon a steady stream of miners had drifted into Last Stand. So far, the finds had been small enough not to attract the interest of mining companies. Most of the people of Last Stand hoped the gold fever would just blow over and not turn their nice little community into a wild mining town. The prospectors tended to be an ornery and independent lot. A new one-bit establishment named the Corner Saloon had already opened up to cater to them, causing Gideon and Finnie nothing but headaches and more work. The place specialized in cheap whiskey and bad beer and had brought prostitution back to town.

Mary, Finnie's wife, had recently purchased the Pearl West Saloon after it had closed. She had converted it into the Last Stand Dance Hall to add to her other thriving businesses, Last Stand Last Chance Saloon and Mary's Place Café. The miners caused the dance girls fits with their grabby hands and forward ways.

"Thank God, they stay out of the Last Chance for the most part. I would be riled if they ruined the place," Doc said.

"Mary makes them toe the mark," Finnie added.

"I wish the town council would let me hire another deputy. This spending Friday and Saturday nights in town is getting old real quick. I'd rather be at home with Abby and the kids tonight," Gideon complained.

"You won't get a new deputy until one of the council gets the daylights scared out of him when you and Finnie aren't around." Doc held the walking stick between his legs and bounced it on the floor.

Finnie reached over and grabbed the cane to stop the noise. "I'm going to hide that thing if you don't stop."

"And I'm liable to see whether the brass or your head is the harder of the two dense materials."

Finnie looked up at Henry, standing beside his grandfather. "Learn everything you can from this old man when it comes to medicine and forget all you see when it comes to his bedside manner. I've tangled with hornet nests that weren't as vicious as this old codger."

Gideon stood and grabbed his hat off the desk. "Henry and I are going to the café for supper. You two are welcome as long as you behave yourselves."

As Doc rose from his seat, he gave Gideon a dirty look. "I brought you into this world and I don't need a lecture from you on manners. Now, let's go. I'm hungry."

The men walked down to Mary's Place and took their seats.

Charlotte Bell came charging toward the table. The waitress was tall for a woman and as skinny as a rail, giving her the appearance of being all arms and legs. While no one had ever described Charlotte as pretty, her outgoing personality made her hard not to be attracted to, nonetheless. "I saw Sam this morning. That little boy of yours gets cuter by the day," she said to Finnie. "Thank God, he has Mary's black hair and not that carrot color of yours, or your big honking Irish nose either. You must be like those stud horses that are a disappointment when they don't pass down their traits to their progeny."

As Gideon and Doc chuckled and Henry looked on in surprise, Finnie slapped the table and said, "Remind me again why Gideon and I rescued you from that arranged marriage? Cecil Hobbs has to be the only man that will ever want to marry you. You'll be living above my saloon forever."

"It's not your saloon – it's Mary's. You don't own anything but a horse. Today's special is meatloaf, browned potatoes, and carrots," Charlotte replied nonchalantly.

Gideon and Doc both shoved their fists against their mouths to stifle laughs for fear of really offending their friend. Finnie shook his head but held his tongue. It was a rare day when someone bested him with their banter, but he begrudgingly knew Charlotte had whipped him but good.

"I'll have the special," Doc said, changing the subject.

Charlotte wasn't through yet and turned her attention to Henry. "If you ever get tired of spending all your time with old men, come look me up. I'm sure we could find something more interesting to talk about than their yapping about the weather and all their aches and pains."

Henry was taken aback by the forward waitress. He stammered a moment and then ordered the special.

Gideon and Finnie also ordered the special. As they waited for the food, they teased Henry about Charlotte until Gideon switched topics and started fawning about his and Abby's two-month-old granddaughter, Elizabeth.

Before Gideon could say too much about the infant, Charlotte delivered the food without hurling any further insults, and the hungry men ate their meals in silence. When they finished, Doc and Finnie went off to play checkers, while Gideon decided to make a walk around the town before the prospectors arrived to begin making their mischief.

Gideon wanted some time alone to think, so he headed toward the residential area of town, away from the businesses. He didn't really believe in intuition, but he had a bad feeling about Fred Parsons's escape from prison. The thought that he might again confront a man who had once saved his life filled him with dread. Try as he might, Gideon couldn't quite get his head around the notion that Fred was an outlaw, even though he knew it was true. On days like this, he sometimes wished he'd never been elected sheriff. Abby and her ranch hand, String Callow, had started to see some encouraging results with her cattle herd. Sometimes, Gideon wished he worked with them instead of administering the law. Cows didn't shoot at you, but, on the other hand, he reminded himself, a bull had once gored his leg and he had almost bled to death.

As Gideon returned to the main street, he noticed several horses already tied to the rail in front of the Last Chance. The local cowboys seldom gave him trouble anymore. They were content to drink in the saloon and then maybe head to the dance hall. It also helped that the prospectors tended to give the gun-wielding ranch hands a wide berth. The trail herd crews, when they were passing through, were often a source of problems, but with the expansion of the rail lines, they were almost a thing of the past. As the sun began to sink to the west, Gideon took a seat beside Henry in front of the jail next to Finnie and Doc while they played checkers.

By nine o'clock, the town was filled with cowboys and prospectors. The saloons and dance hall were loud with all the laughter and conversations, mostly carried on in near yelling voices. Gideon and Finnie had drifted down to the Last Chance Saloon and were drinking beers at a table. They had taken turns making appearances in the other saloon and the dance hall but had yet to encounter any trouble.

Two gunshots from across the street caused the patrons of the Last Chance to go silent as they all looked toward the windows. Gideon and Finnie made a dash for the door. As they reached the street, a third shot rang out from inside the Corner Saloon. The lawmen drew their weapons and ran into the building. An old, white-haired prospector with a beard down to his bellybutton waved an ancient rusty Colt Navy pistol. He spun toward the door when he noticed all the other patrons looking that way.

"Old-timer, you need to set that gun on the floor right now before anybody gets hurt," Gideon warned.

The prospector wobbled toward the lawmen. "What are you going to do about it if I don't? I fought in the war, and I know how to kill," he bellowed.

Gideon took a couple of steps to the side to separate himself from Finnie in hopes of distracting the miner and providing the deputy with a chance to subdue the old man. "You shoot that gun again and you'll be dead. You can't get both of us. Now, be a good sport and put the gun down – please."

The miner laughed. "I got the sheriff begging me."

Finnie charged like a raging bull and drove his short oxlike body into the miner. As he landed on top of the man, the prospector let out a loud groan like the bawling of a sick cow. Gideon ran up and pinned the miner's arm with his boot before retrieving the gun.

"Nice work, Finnie," Gideon said as he helped the Irishman to his feet.

"Drunken old man," Finnie muttered as he yanked the miner to his feet. The prospector was in too much pain to offer any resistance.

"Is anybody hurt?" Gideon called out.

"He shot into the ceiling," the bartender answered.

"You better go make sure he didn't kill any of your whores."

The bartender disappeared up the stairs and returned a few moments later. "Everybody is fine, but one of the customers wants a refund. Says he didn't finish proper," the bartender said with a laugh.

Gideon failed to find any humor in the situation. "Everybody better behave themselves for the rest of the night. If I have to come in here again, it's not going to be pretty," he warned before they walked the miner out of the saloon.

As they were walking across the street toward the jail, Gideon sensed someone approaching from behind him. He drew his Colt and spun around. A little Indian boy dropped to the ground and covered his head.

"Where in tarnation did he come from?" Gideon asked.

"He's mine," the prospector said as he looked over his shoulder.

"You have a son that young? He looks full-blooded Indian to me," Finnie said warily.

"No, I just found him roaming around in the woods. He's been helping me pan for gold."

Gideon helped the boy to his feet and took his hand. "This boy can't be over eight years old. You mean to tell me he was just out wandering on his own? I don't know of any Indians still living around here. What's his name?"

"I just call him boy. He was scavenging for food when I found him. He don't talk American."

Gideon and Finnie exchanged skeptical looks.

"Oh, I bet he talks American just fine. English is probably a different matter," Gideon said. "When's the last time he ate?"

"He had a bit of breakfast," the prospector answered.

"I ought to take a whip to you," Gideon said. He shoved the miner toward the jail.

Once they were inside, Finnie took the miner to the cell room and locked him up. When he came back into the office, he asked, "What are we going to do?"

"Did you learn any of the Ute language when you had your squaw?" Gideon asked.

"She spoke English fairly well. I knew a few words, but I never really had a knack for learning it, and I certainly don't remember them now. That was in another lifetime."

"That's no help. Would you go over to the café and get him a plate of food? Charge it to the county. I'll make the boy a pallet. He can sleep here with me tonight."

"Sure, I can do that."

"Finnie, something isn't right about this. We can sort this out in the morning, but things just don't add up," Gideon said as he tossed his hat onto the desk.

"I was thinking the same thing. We can keep that old fart locked up until he tells us the truth though."

"That, my friend, is the wisest thing you've said all day."

Chapter 2

The rising sun's light coming through the jail window provided just enough illumination for Gideon to make out the features of the room. His night spent on the cot had made for fitful sleeping. Truth be told, he never slept well anymore unless Abby's leg was draped across his own and she was snoring softly in his ear. For a man that had spent nearly his entire life sleeping alone, the notion he needed his wife beside him now to rest, both amused and annoyed him. Gideon got up and checked on the still sleeping Indian boy before making coffee. By the time he was drinking his second cup, Finnie dragged into the office.

"I'm getting too old to stay up all night trying to get cowboys and miners to behave themselves," Finnie said as he poured a cup of coffee.

"I know it. And too old to sleep on that cot," Gideon said, grimacing at the sight of the bed.

"You should just move to town. It would simplify your life considerably."

"I wouldn't be happy in town and Abby would kill me if I even mentioned it. Her and String are mighty proud of that herd of cattle."

"They have a right to be. There aren't many women ranchers around here. You should be proud of her, too." Finnie took his usual seat, nearly spilling his coffee in the process.

"You know I am. I don't even know why you said that. Sometimes I think you enjoy riling me just to relieve boredom."

Finnie grinned. "What do you want me to do with the old man?"

"Just what you said. Walk away if he doesn't tell you the truth about the boy."

"I'll drink some coffee first and feed the boy before I bother," Finnie said, then slurped noisily from his cup.

The boy was just starting to stir when the door to the jail flung open. Finnie's wife, Mary, came barreling in with Sam in her arms. The soon to be two-year-old was screaming at the top of his lungs. Mary was crying too. Her eyes were red, and her black hair was pasted to a trail of tears running down her cheeks.

"What is it? Is Sam hurt?" Finnie hollered as he arose to meet his wife.

"Charlotte . . ." Mary stammered. "Charlotte is dead."

Finnie embraced his wife and child as Mary began sobbing uncontrollably. She tried talking, but whatever she said came out indecipherable. Finnie remained stoic at first, but his façade began to crack like a window under assault from a hailstorm. He buried his face in Mary's neck and began weeping.

Gideon was too stunned to even move. His legs felt weak as if they might not support his weight anyway. He had liked Charlotte from the moment she had showed up at the jail after running away from an arranged marriage, but his relationship with the girl paled in comparison to that of Finnie and Mary toward her. Charlotte was family to them – a surrogate bratty little sister they adored. The only thing Gideon could do was wait for Mary to calm down to learn what had happened. He glanced over at the Indian boy who had curled up in the corner of the jail, watching the drama unfold.

Finnie and Mary finally gained some sense of composure and even Sam quieted down. The deputy led his wife over to a chair and sat down beside her.

"Tell us what happened," Finnie said gently.

"I needed to work on the ledger, so I took Sam to the saloon. Charlotte is always up early so I figured she could play with him while I worked. She wasn't in the back room eating breakfast like usual, so I went up to her room to check on her. When I saw the bed made and that she wasn't in there, I got concerned. I found her in the café stabbed to death," Mary said and started crying again.

Gideon watched as the color left Finnie's face. The knowledge that Charlotte had been murdered was a hard thing to comprehend. As Gideon stood, he couldn't help but think of the fear the girl must have felt as she died. "Mary, I hate to ask this, but will you stay here and keep an eye on that boy. I don't want him wandering off," he said, pointing toward the corner.

Mary spun her head around, seeing the Indian boy for the first time. "Sure, I can do that," she said between sniffles.

"Finnie, let's go and get this over with."

When they got into the street, Finnie said, "Maybe we should get Doc, just in case."

"Yeah, maybe we should."

Doc realized that something was gravely wrong as soon as the men walked into the room. "What is it?" he asked, trepidation in his voice.

"Mary found Charlotte stabbed to death. We thought you should come," Gideon said.

"Oh, my God," Doc said and rubbed his hand over his mouth. He leaned back in his chair to collect himself a moment before jumping up to retrieve his medical bag. "Henry, you stay here." He followed the lawmen out the door.

Gideon stationed Finnie and Doc outside of the front door and walked around back to the alley. Any hopes he had of finding tracks were quickly dashed by the amount of traffic the road had these days. The alley was covered in horse and foot prints. At the back entrance, the doorjamb was busted from the door being kicked in. He stepped inside and saw Charlotte lying on her back in the kitchen area with her feet pointed toward the rear entrance. A kitchen knife protruded from her chest and a massive amount of blood surrounded the body. Her eyes were open as if she were staring up at the ceiling. Gideon had to put a hand against the wall to steady himself from the sight. "Come on in," he bellowed.

Doc and Finnie walked through the front of the building and into the kitchen. Finnie took one look at Charlotte and bolted for the front door.

As Doc squatted next to the body, he said, "It would take the lowest form of human debauchery to do this to a young girl. Poor Charlotte. This was a cruel and painful death. I can't imagine the fear she felt."

"Maybe I better go check on Finnie."

"Nah, just give him some time alone to gather himself. You can be there for him later."

"I don't know why they thought they had to kill her. As scrawny as she was, just about any man could have overpowered her and tied her up."

"Some people just get a thrill out of killing. Maybe somebody in town last night saw something out of the ordinary," Doc said as he pulled the knife out of Charlotte's body and dropped it to the floor.

"I can only hope. They must have waited until she closed at ten and then kicked the door in as she cleaned. I guess I should check the cashbox," Gideon said as he stepped around the body and into the front. "It's empty."

"They took her necklace that Finnie and Mary got her for Christmas and that little gold ring she wore."

"What a lowlife bastard."

"We need to get a stretcher and carry Charlotte to my office. I doubt I'll learn anything more than I already know, but you never can tell. Your killer was left-handed," Doc said as he stood.

"You can tell that?"

"Sure. Look at how most of the wounds are on the right side of her torso and at the angle of entry. A right-handed wound would tilt just opposite."

"I see what you mean. That's good work and it'll eliminate most people," Gideon said as he bounded for the door. "I'll be back shortly with a stretcher and a blanket."

By the time they carried Charlotte's body into the doctor's office, the townsfolk were hustling down the boardwalk spreading gossip of a possible murder in Last Stand. Once the body was placed on the table, Doc shooed the lawmen out of his office before he began his examination of the body.

"Don't you think Henry should come with us?" Finnie asked as he paused at the door.

Doc glanced at his ashen-colored grandson until looking back at Finnie. "I appreciate your thoughtfulness, I truly do, but if Henry wants to be a doctor, he needs to see such things. It's better to find out if he has the stomach for it now rather than later. You boys go on and I'll stop by the jail later."

As the lawmen stopped on the boardwalk outside of Doc's office, Gideon said, "Finnie, I'm really sorry about Charlotte. I know she meant a lot to you."

Finnie had to look away before speaking. "Nothing for you to be sorry about. The one that did this will be the sorry one when I get my hands on him. Robbing the café is one thing, but there was no call to kill her. That was just plain meanness."

"Doc says whoever did it was left-handed."

"Really? Fred's left-handed."

"I remember. You don't really think he's sunk that low, do you?" Gideon asked.

"I sure hope not because I'll show him no loyalty if he did."

"We better check on Mary. I don't know what to expect from that boy."

Inside the jail, Mary sat on the floor with Sam and the Indian boy. Sam had taken a shine to the boy and was playing with him.

Mary turned to face the men, and in a solemn voice, she asked, "What did you find?"

"Not much yet. We need to ask around and see if anybody saw anything unusual," Gideon replied.

Mary squeezed her lips together and inhaled loudly as she steeled herself from crying. "Charlotte was like family," she said, her voice breaking.

"I know she was. We'll find who did this," Gideon assured her.

"I'm going to check on the prospector," Finnie said.

"Stick to our plan," Gideon reminded him.

Finnie returned a moment later. "He's still saying he found the boy. What are we going to do with the child? This makes for a poor place to keep him."

Mary stood and straightened her skirt. "He can come home with us. I'm not going to the saloon today. I'd run off all the customers with my crying."

Finnie pulled his head and shoulders back in surprise. "Mary, that boy is an Indian. You don't know what he's capable of doing."

"Nonsense. He's a sweet little boy. Nobody has taught him to hate yet. We'll be fine. And his name is Cany."

"He understands English?" Gideon asked in surprise.

"No. I pointed at myself and said my name and then I pointed at Sam and said his. Cany understood immediately what I meant and said his name," Mary said.

Still skeptical, Finnie asked, "Are you sure about this?"

"I am. He's good with Sam. He's just a little boy wrapped in darker skin than we are. Sam and Cany will help me keep my mind off all this. You know I loved Charlotte just like she was my sister."

Gideon ran his fingers through his hair before returning his hat to his head. "I guess I better ride out to Paradise and tell Charlotte's parents. I'm sure I'll be blamed for her death for getting her out of that place."

Charlotte had come from a religious commune named Paradise. After a scandal and the demise of their leader, the community had fallen apart. Some of the people had stayed and continued ranching and farming, but many had moved away in shame.

"Charlotte's parents moved back to Ohio. Even after Pastor Gordon was found a fraud, they still never forgave Charlotte for not marrying Cecil. Her father told her he never wanted to see her again," Mary said.

"I'll send a telegram to the sheriff in Toledo. Maybe he can track them down. They at least deserve to know she's gone," Gideon said.

"Just find who did this. I'm headed home. Don't worry about us," Mary said as she picked up Sam and took Cany by the hand. She gave Finnie a kiss before leaving.

Gideon sat down at his desk. "This afternoon, when the prospectors and ranch hands come to town, we'll go talk to them and see if anybody saw something."

"Let's hope so. I guess I better go clean up the café and fix the door," Finnie said.

"Wait until we hear from Doc and then I'll help you. We probably should look around one more time anyway."

An hour later, Doc entered the jail and took a seat. "Well, Charlotte wasn't raped. She didn't have to suffer that indignity anyway. That girl fought like a cornered mountain lion. Her hands are all cut up from trying to defend herself against the knife and she has a couple of broken fingernails. I would think her attacker has some scratch marks. That's about all I can add. I had the undertaker come get her body."

"Thanks, Doc. That's better than nothing," Gideon said.

Finnie stopped his pacing and sat down beside the doctor. "Mary and I need to get a family plot in the cemetery. Charlotte can be buried there so she won't be alone forever."

"I think she'd like that," Doc said. "She can torment you after your death then."

The Irishman smiled for the first time. "That she can. It would be fine by me. Where's your annoying walking cane?"

"I put it up. Charlotte never liked me using it. She was always afraid I'd get dependent on that thing and get feeble. I'm doing it for her," Doc replied.

"How did Henry hold up?" Finnie asked.

"He got a little green around the gills, but he did just fine. I'm proud of him. He helped me and learned a thing or two."

"Aye, a chip off the old block."

Gideon grabbed his hat. "Let's go look around some more and then clean the café."

After spending time once again inspecting the café and the alley, and finding nothing, Gideon and Finnie scrubbed away the blood. The wood floor was left with a permanent stain that would forever be a reminder of Charlotte and what had happened there. Once they finished the cleaning, they repaired the door.

By the time the lawmen had eaten lunch at the Last Chance Saloon, the town was abuzz with the news of Charlotte's murder. With it being Saturday, the cowboys and miners began arriving shortly afterward. Gideon and Finnie spent the rest of the day talking to as many people as possible. While nobody had seen anything unusual, the influx of all the new prospectors made it difficult for folks to know if any strangers had been in town the previous night.

At five o'clock, Gideon said, "Finnie, you need to go home and be with Mary tonight. She'll need company. I can handle any unruly drunks by myself."

Finnie furled his brow at the suggestion. "What if you encounter another situation like last night?"

"I'll just shoot them tonight and ask questions later. I'm in no mood for shenanigans."

"Are you sure?"

"Yes, just feed our prisoner in the morning. Don't release him even if he tells you where he got the boy. We'll hold him to Monday. I want to talk to him one way or the other. I'm going home after the saloons close."

"Gideon, thanks for letting me go home."

Gideon threw his arm around Finnie. "Go take care of your family. That's all any of us really has at the end of the day."

Chapter 3

The smell of bacon frying aroused Gideon from a slumber in which he dreamed of his dead granddaughter, Tess. He climbed out of bed and got dressed still hungover with melancholy from the dream. Downstairs, Gideon found Abby turning the bacon over in the skillet. He walked up behind her and kissed her on the back of the neck. "Good morning, Mrs. Johann."

"A good morning to you, too. It's nice seeing you again," Abby said with a touch of sarcasm.

When Gideon and Abby had renewed their romance after all the years apart, she had told him she would support him in whatever he wanted to do with his life, but she had come to hate the times when his job kept him away from home. There were days where she wished Gideon wasn't the sheriff. They had spent enough years apart, and she didn't want to waste another day away from each other. And besides that, the job was much more perilous than she had ever imagined.

"Abby, I've got some bad news."

Abby thought Gideon was teasing her in response to what she had said. "Oh, really? And what may that be?" she asked playfully.

"Charlotte was murdered."

The news caused Abby to drop the fork into the skillet with a clatter. She spun around and looked Gideon in the eyes before burying her face into his chest. "Why would anybody harm that poor girl? She'd been through enough in her life already."

"Somebody robbed the café after it closed. I don't know why they felt the need to kill her. Charlotte fought them to the end. Maybe she infuriated them or maybe they just liked killing. I don't know. Finnie and Mary are beside themselves."

"I feel for them. They really took Charlotte under their wing. I'm going to miss her, too." Abby quickly wiping her eyes as the children entered the room.

Winnie, Abby's daughter from a previous marriage, was thirteen. Puberty was hitting her hard and causing her to be a moody teenager. She had always been a willful child and the onset of womanhood was not making her any less so. On her good days, she and her mother could enjoy their maturing relationship with frank conversations about life, and on the bad days, Winnie could be more temperamental and prone to crying than her nearly four-year-old brother, Chance.

Chance was all boy and spoiled rotten by his two sisters. His deep blue eyes, inherited from his father, twinkled with mischievousness. He talked nonstop and liked to spend his time outside roughhousing with his dog, Red.

"What's the matter?" Winnie asked as she sat down at the table.

"Nothing. Everything is fine," Abby replied.

Winnie sensed immediately from her mother's failure to make eye contact that she was lying. Panic tightened her chest and caused her to catch her breath at the thought that something might be wrong with her baby niece, Elizabeth. She still occasionally had nightmares stemming from when her first niece, Tess, had died. "It's Elizabeth, isn't it? Is she dead?" she cried out.

"No, no, honey. Elizabeth is fine. Charlotte from the café died," Abby answered.

"Oh. That makes me sad. She was nice. She always gave Chance and me a lemon drop after our meals. What happened? She's awfully young to be dying."

Gideon and Abby exchanged glances until the smell of bacon starting to burn forced Abby to turn back to the stove.

"The café was robbed, and she was murdered. I'm going to find the person that did it and arrest them," Gideon said as he took a seat.

The news upset Winnie. She leaned back in her chair and began rubbing her forehead. "Why? Why would somebody hurt a nice person like Charlotte? The world is full of bad men. We're all going to get killed."

Gideon reached over and took Winnie by the hand. "No, most people are good. The bad ones just stand out because of the evil they do. I'll keep you all safe. Now quit your worrying. The only thing you need to concern yourself with is keeping Benjamin Oakes from kissing you. He'll make you have pimples," he said in an attempt to lighten the moment.

Benjamin was the son of Gideon's best friend, Ethan. He and Winnie were the same age and had known each other all their lives. Their mutual fascination with each other had led to endless debates amongst Ethan's church congregation as to whether the children were practically siblings or destined for a life together.

"You don't have to worry about that anymore. Benjamin has been all shy lately like we just met. He's always staring at me and not saying anything. I don't know what's wrong with him," Winnie answered, her attention successfully diverted away from Charlotte's death.

"Sometimes you have to lead a horse to water," Gideon teased.

Abby turned toward the table with a plate of slightly burned bacon and a bowl of scrambled eggs. "That particular horse can just stay thirsty awhile longer until he's old enough to find the water for himself. Everybody, eat up so we can get ready for church. We will not be late."

After rushing the family through the meal, Abby dressed Chance and then got herself ready as Gideon hitched up the buckboard. The family arrived at the church with plenty of time to spare. Most of the church members were milling about outside. Some of them had already heard of Charlotte's death, and the subject now seemed to be on everybody's tongue as Gideon walked up to Ethan while Abby headed toward Ethan's wife, Sarah.

"That's terrible about Charlotte," Ethan said, his relationship with Gideon so long and deep that greetings were not necessary.

Ethan Oakes was a successful rancher that preached on Sundays. With his towering height and broad shoulders, he dwarfed his skinny friend. In the last year, he had finally talked Sarah into building a nice house to replace their cabin that had become too small with the addition of their adopted daughter, Sylvia. Ethan was a calm and thoughtful man that balanced out Gideon's more impulsive nature.

"Finnie and Mary are taking it hard. I don't imagine they will be here today. And to top it off, I don't have a clue on who did it other than they were left-handed," Gideon said.

"I'll have to go check on Finnie and Mary. I feel for them, and of course for Charlotte, too. She was a fine girl. I guess the quiet times were bound to end. It's been right at a year since anything bad has happened around here."

"Well, I would have been fine going another year with breaking up bar fights as my biggest challenge."

Gideon's son-in-law, Zack, walked up to the men. Zack stood almost as tall as Ethan though it wasn't nearly as stocky. His face looked puffy and his shoulders sagged.

"You look like hell," Gideon said and smiled. He had come to love Zack like a son and had no reservations on what he would say to him. The young man was a good person and had proven himself in action enough times for Gideon to know he was as brave as any man alive. He also admired Zack for putting up with his spitfire daughter, Joann.

Joann had been born out of wedlock to Gideon and Abby after he had left for the war. He had never known of the child until he returned to Last Stand eighteen years later. All the family had been overjoyed when Joann delivered a healthy baby girl in April after previously losing a child in infancy that had nearly destroyed the young mother.

"If you want me looking pretty then you need to tell your granddaughter that nighttime is for sleeping," Zack said, causing the men to chuckle.

"It doesn't last forever. Just remind yourself of that on the bad nights," Ethan assured the young father.

"Oh, I know. I'm just thankful Elizabeth is healthy. Joann seems to have quit stressing about the baby. Those first few weeks she nearly worried herself to death that something bad was going to happen, like it did with Tess. I was afraid she was going to get like she was before, but she's back to being her bratty self," Zack said, grinning.

Gideon shook his head and smiled. "I don't want to hear about it. You knew full well what you were getting yourself into when you married Joann. It wasn't as if she pretended to be what she wasn't. You just kept running back for more."

Ethan nudged Gideon with his elbow. "Remember that time we were chopping wood and Zack rode up and threw his hat on the ground and said he wanted nothing to do with her ever again. He got all mad at us for trying to give him some advice."

The two men broke into laughter as Zack colored with embarrassment at the memory.

"You two are just hilarious. Both of you riled me up on purpose that day," Zack protested.

"I'm going to walk over and see my grandbaby," Gideon said as he headed toward Abby, Joann, and Sarah. Ethan and Zack followed.

Abby held the sleeping baby while Sarah comforted Joann as she cried from just having learned of Charlotte's death. Gideon held out his arms and his wife passed him Elizabeth. He smiled at his grandchild and ran his finger down her delicate nose. Holding Elizabeth sure beat thinking about the murder.

"Isn't she a doll baby?" Abby marveled.

"Yes, she is. She looks like she sleeps just fine to me. Her mean old daddy is telling stories on this precious baby," Gideon cooed.

While wiping her eyes, Joann let out a snort. "She's sleeping just fine now because she stayed up all night. That little thing is wearing Zack and me out."

"Abby and I can bring the kids and stay over so you and Zack can get a good night of sleep," Gideon offered.

Gideon's comment caused Sarah to burst into laughter in spite of the sadness hanging in the air.

Looking up from the baby with a puzzled look on his face, Gideon asked, "What's so funny?"

"You are. I was just standing here reminiscing about the bitter, mad at the world, shot to pieces man that convalesced in my home a few years ago. It's hard to reconcile him with the one grinning like a fool at his grandbaby now," Sarah said with an impish grin.

Gideon had never intended to return to Last Stand. Ethan and Sarah's son, Benjamin, had found him near dead from getting shot by the cattle rustlers he was chasing. The family and Doc Abram had nursed him back to health. Sarah was not from Last Stand, and Gideon had never met her until his return. Her belief that he could put his past behind him and start over had played a huge role in his life being what it was today. Sarah, never one to mince words, had set Gideon straight on more than one occasion. He thought of her as his sister and would do anything for her.

"And this is the thanks I get for listening to you back then," Gideon said, smiling.

Ethan put his arm around Sarah. "All right, you two, it's time for church. We had better get inside before

Gideon begins sulking. We all know he's a baby when he gets his feelings hurt."

Gideon did not speak but just shook his head with a sardonic grin as he passed Elizabeth to Joann.

Chapter 4

As Gideon walked into the jail on Monday morning, he found Finnie drinking coffee and singing an Irish tune while he inventoried their ammunition. Through the shut door to the cell room, Gideon could hear the prospector raising holy hell.

Finnie looked up from his work. "Our miner is apparently ready to talk," he said wryly.

"Have you talked to him?" Gideon asked as he poured a cup of coffee.

"You said you wanted to talk to him, so I waited. He is starting to get on my nerves though."

"Why didn't you talk to him just to shut him up?"

Finnie shrugged his shoulders. "It's like what the ugly whore that had been passed over all night said when asked why she didn't get in line when the next cowboy walked in. What's the point?"

Gideon shook his head in dismay and was about to ask about Mary when he decided he'd heard all the hollering he could take. He grabbed the water bucket used to make coffee and flung the door to the cell room open. With the sweep of the bucket, he doused the prospector with the water. "Shut up and I'll talk with you directly. If I hear another word from you before then, I'll cut out your tongue." He shut the door and took a seat at his desk.

"Wish I'd thought of that," Finnie muttered.

"How is Mary holding up?"

Finnie took his usual seat across the desk from Gideon. "She's doing all right. She has her moments where she has a good cry, but you know how strong that woman is. Mary is a trooper."

"And yourself?"

Shrugging again, Finnie then rubbed his chin a moment before speaking. "You and I have seen a lot of death, and we're still fighting the good fight, but this one is hard – I'm not going to lie. I'm going to miss Charlotte. She and Doc are about the only two that can win a war of words with me."

Gideon smiled sadly. "That she could. I'm going to miss her, too. If I can do anything for either of you, just let me know. You know I'll do my best."

"I know. Ethan and Sarah came by yesterday afternoon. We're going to do the funeral at the church tomorrow. I have to go pick out a family plot here in a little while and arrange to have the grave dug."

Nodding his head until stopping abruptly, Gideon said, "I almost forgot. How is the Indian boy doing?"

"Cany is doing fine. He's a good boy. We don't communicate so well, but we get by. He's really no trouble, and in fact, he keeps Sam occupied so Mary can get some things done."

"That's good. I guess I better go talk to that old-timer," Gideon said as he stood.

When the lawmen entered the cell room, the prospector yelled, "You had no right to throw water on me or to hold me this long. I've got gold to pan."

Gideon pulled out his knife and started cleaning his fingernails, causing the old man to back up against the wall. "I'm in no mood for your mouth. Answer my questions or I'll leave you to rot in here. I really don't give a damn. Now, where did you get that boy?"

The prospector looked down at his feet for a moment before meeting the sheriff's gaze. "Two men showed up at my camp with the boy on the back of one of their horses. They sold him to me for fifty dollars. Said he could do the work of most men and they weren't lying," he replied.

"Where did they get him?"

"I don't have a clue. I didn't ask questions. I'm not the only miner with a boy. Several of them have one now."

Gideon and Finnie exchanged glances at the comment.

"Why did you bring the boy to town?" Finnie asked.

"I found a couple of nuggets that day and I didn't want to cash them out in front of the other prospectors. That's a good way to get your throat slashed or your claim jumped. I was afraid the boy would steal them while I was in town, so I brought him with me. Seems like kind of a bad idea now."

Gideon unlocked the door to the cell. "Get out of here."

"What about my boy?" the miner asked as he stepped out of the cell.

"He's not yours. It's against the law to own a slave. Now scat."

"I want my fifty dollars for him then."

With a move so swift that even Finnie jumped, Gideon grabbed the miner by the throat and pinned him against the bars to the cell. "I don't like you. If you ever even so much as look at me wrong, I'll beat you so badly you'll never be able to hold a pan in your hands again. Do you understand?"

The miner couldn't speak and could barely nod his head with the hand gripping his throat. When Gideon released him, he bolted out of the jail.

"I kind of suspected he bought or stole that boy, but I sure as hell didn't expect him to say there were more boys out there," Gideon said as they walked back into the office area.

"Me either," Finnie added.

Gideon dropped into his chair with enough force to make it groan from the strain. "Now we're going to have to concern ourselves with finding Charlotte's murderer and rounding up Indian boys. And I don't know what we'll do with the boys after we find them. They had to come from somewhere."

"They have to be from the Southern Ute Reservation. That's the only place there'd be enough Indian boys to supply a kidnap ring unless they're traveling from a long ways. I'm sure Cany is a Ute. I've been around enough of them to know one when I see one."

"What do you want to do with him until we get this straightened out?"

"We can keep him. He's really no trouble."

"What are we going to do with the rest of them?" Gideon asked, the weight of his question causing him to rub his scar in concern.

"Maybe we need to go talk to the Indian agent and find out what's going on before we round anybody up. We best know where the boys come from first."

"That's a good point, Finnie. Do you know where the agency is at?"

"It's at Ignacio. That's about twenty miles southeast of Animas City. Well, I guess actually Durango now. Did you know the railroad built a station a couple miles south of Animas City and the whole town picked up and moved to what's now Durango? I hear tell Animas City is a ghost town now."

The mention of Animas City made Gideon smile. He'd found Finnie there serving as the town drunk after the two men hadn't seen each other in years. Finnie hadn't had a drop of whiskey since Mary had told him to pick her or the whiskey.

"Animas City didn't go under because of the railroad. They went under because their town drunk up and moved here," Gideon joked.

Finnie chuckled and slapped his leg. "You may have a point there."

"Do you know anybody around here that is married to an Indian woman? Maybe we could find someone to talk to Cany before we head clear down there."

"This is your town, not mine. You should know the answer to that."

"I haven't been back in Last Stand that much longer than you. I can't think of anyone. I'll ask Doc. He'll know."

"That's for sure. That old codger knows everything about everybody," Finnie mused.

"We'll see if we can find somebody to talk to Cany, but the rest will have to wait. I don't want Charlotte's murderer to disappear. Let's go talk to all the business owners and see if anybody has been spending money in a big way."

"I better get the burial plot situation taken care of first and then I'll get to it."

"That's fine. I'll take this side of the street and you can take the other. We'll meet back here when we're through," Gideon said. He stood and headed for the door.

Gideon and Finnie spent all morning talking to townsfolk and hadn't found anyone with any useful information. Most of them had been home and in bed by the time of the murder. Those that had been in the saloons that night kept mentioning it was impossible to know if any stranger had been lurking about the town with all the new prospectors in Last Stand.

At lunch, Gideon asked Doc if he knew of any Ute Indians in the area. The only one the doctor could recall that still lived in the area had been murdered during the scandal with the preacher from Paradise. Gideon headed back to the office resigned to the fact that a trip to see the Indian agent would be necessary.

While sitting around in the jail, Finnie came up with the idea to try sign language with Cany. He admitted he wasn't all that good at it, but he and Gideon walked to Finnie's house, nonetheless. Gideon and Mary watched in fascination as Finnie began signing. Cany's eyes lit up and he began making motions with his hands. For the next couple of minutes, the two of them exchanged hand signals.

After they finished, Finnie blew out his breath in relief that they were done signing. He turned toward Gideon and Mary. "To tell you the truth, Cany isn't any better than me at this, but I learned he was stolen from his people by two men. They took three boys. I couldn't understand from where, though I still think he's Southern Ute. That's really the only useful information I got."

"That's more than we had. I'll take it. Let's get back to work," Gideon said.

By the end of the afternoon, Charlotte's grave had been dug in what was now the Ford family plot. Finnie walked to the cemetery to inspect the hole. He had no complaint with the work and the graveyard provided him with an opportunity to be alone – something he found to be in short supply these days. Charlotte's death had put him in a reflective mood. He thought about his arrival in Last Stand when Gideon had dragged him to town knowing he was dealing with a drunk so far gone that he had the shakes. Gideon and Mary had saved his life. It had been four years since he'd taken a drink of whiskey. Sobriety, marriage, and fatherhood had changed him in ways he could never have imagined. He felt things so deeply these days that it embarrassed him. Sometimes he had to act the fool to keep from getting misty just being with Mary and Sam. As Finnie stared down into the hole in the ground, he felt an emptiness he hadn't felt in a long time. Charlotte had become the most unlikely of family. He was going to miss her for a very long time, and come hell or high water, he would find her killer. With a swipe of his sleeve across his eyes, he spun around to go back to the jail.

As Finnie neared the sheriff's office, he saw Mary also headed there. She spotted him and waited at the door for her husband.

"I was just coming to see you and Gideon," Mary announced.

"Well, Mrs. Ford, you are always most welcome here," Finnie teased.

Mary smiled at Finnie, but she knew her husband well enough to know the comment had been a little forced. Under Finnie's smile, she could see the melancholy that Charlotte's death had brought over him. His caring nature caused a surge of love to course through her. She leaned over and kissed his cheek. With a wink, Finnie opened the door and ushered in his wife.

Gideon, lost in thought, looked up from doodling on a piece of paper and was surprised to see Mary. "Whatever that lying Irishman said about me isn't true," he joked.

"I already knew he was lying because he was singing your praises," Mary retorted.

The exchange caused the three of them to chuckle, relieving the somber mood they all felt.

"Are you getting anywhere with solving the murder?" Mary asked.

Gideon slowly shook his head.

"I want to offer a five-hundred-dollar reward for information leading to the conviction of the killer," Mary stated.

The news caused Gideon to lean back in his chair and to rub his scar. "Let's all take a seat and discuss this."

"Mary, can we afford that?" Finnie asked as he dropped into his chair.

Mary sat down and leaned over, patting Finnie's hand. "Oh, honey, I've kept you in the dark for too long about running our businesses. It was always just easier to handle those things and not bother you with them, but you need to start learning things, especially now that we have the dance hall. But yes, we can afford it."

When Finnie had wed Mary, he'd been too intimidated by her success in running the Last Chance Saloon to dare ask her about her income. The subject had never once come up in conversation since then and he was content with the arrangement. Mary, for her part, had realized how uncomfortable Finnie was with the fact his wife made substantially more money than he did. She had avoided the situation until it had become a subject they never broached.

"Whether you can afford it or not, that's a lot of money. I hate to see you do that. We should be able to solve this ourselves," Gideon said.

"Nonsense. I want to. That's the least I can do for Charlotte. She deserves that much if it will help. There's nothing like money to encourage a little cooperation," Mary said.

Gideon looked over at Finnie. "How do you feel about it?"

"I'm all for it. I won't rest until we serve justice," Finnie answered with a nod of the head.

"Well, let's head to the printer and get some posters made. Mary, thank you," Gideon said.

Mary nodded her head. Her eyes were starting to well with tears. "God, I loved that gangly girl. I need to go see Doc."

Dating back to her time as a prostitute, Mary had always had a special bond with the doctor. During those days, he had been her only true confidante. Doc had provided her the shoulder to cry on as she had adjusted to life as a whore while still mourning the murder of her husband, Eugene. And Doc had never been judgmental with her or treated her any differently than he would have any other woman. In time, he had come to confide in her, too.

"Mary, what can I do for you?" Doc asked when he saw her come through his doorway.

"Doc, I need to talk to you," Mary answered.

Doc looked over at his grandson. "Henry, would you mind going for a walk?"

"Sure," Henry replied.

"Henry, I'm sorry for running you off," Mary said.

"That's all right. I need some fresh air anyway."

"How are you doing?" Doc asked after Henry walked outside.

"Doc, I feel as if I barely have the strength to go on. I can't get it out of my head thinking about the fear Charlotte must have felt as she fought for her life. She was so dear to me."

"I know she was. Mary, you are probably the strongest person I know. You've been through more in your short life than most people endure into old age, and you always kept going with your best foot forward. You'll do the same thing this time. Healing from a loss like this takes time. You know that from when you lost Eugene. You got through that and you'll get through this. Finnie and Sam need you. And you know I'm always here for you."

Mary forced a smile as she dabbed at her eyes with a handkerchief. "Sometimes I think it would be better to be weak and just let life kick me around instead of fighting it."

"That's pure nonsense. You know it wouldn't. And besides, you couldn't do that even if you wanted to. It's just not in your nature. You're a fighter until your last breath. That's why I love you."

"I think you give me more credit than I deserve, but I appreciate your support. I always feel better after talking to you. Life goes on I guess, and I do have Finnie and Sam to look after, but the café is sure not going to be the same without Charlotte in it teasing all our customers."

Chapter 5

Ethan Oakes stood at the pulpit looking out at a packed room in attendance for Charlotte's funeral. Many of the folks were from town and even a few were from what was left of the Paradise commune. Almost none of these people ever came to Ethan's church. The size of the crowd surprised him. He would have never guessed Charlotte could have touched so many lives with her job as a waitress.

Raising his arms, palms outward, to quiet the noise, Ethan said, "Thank you all for coming. We're here today to celebrate and remember the life of Charlotte Bell. I didn't know Charlotte all that well, but the times I was around her, I found it a joy to be in her company. She always struck me as a kind and thoughtful person. Her ability to have the last word with our loquacious Deputy Finnie Ford is enough to make her legendary in these here parts of Colorado." The comment brought a chuckle from the crowd and made Finnie smile.

Ethan continued talking about Charlotte's life. As he drew near the end of his eulogy, he said, "Most people would say that Charlotte is in a better place. As Christians, we accept this as a matter of faith. And while I would never argue this point, I will say I think some of us get there way too quickly – Charlotte certainly did. This world would surely be a better place with her still in it. All of us must do our best to root out the evil we see for all the Charlottes of this world." He led the mourners in a prayer and then turned the pulpit over to anybody that wanted to say a few words.

Mary got up to speak. "I don't know how much most of you know about me, and there are parts of my life I hope you have forgotten," she began, causing a mixed reaction to her reference she had been a prostitute after her first husband had been murdered until she inherited the Last Chance. "I was an orphan, so family is not something I take for granted. My family is all the people that have been kind enough to include me in their world. Charlotte was one of those people. Our relationship started out kind of rocky with her religious upbringing and my running a saloon, but that all changed fairly quickly, and we became sisters. For Finnie and me, she was like the precocious little sister that neither of us had. I loved her dearly and will remember her the rest of my life . . ." Her voice broke. "I love you, Charlotte."

As Mary scuttled back to her seat, she stumbled and nearly fell to the floor. She rushed to her seat and buried her face in her hands, unable to control her emotions. Her sobs were loud and sounded as if she couldn't catch her breath. Finnie threw his arm around his wife and pulled her against his chest.

When no one else chose to speak, Ethan led the crowd in reciting the Lord's Prayer. As the lid was placed on the coffin, Joann bolted for the door, clutching Elizabeth so tightly that the baby began to cry. The commotion caused the crowd to all turn to see what was happening. Zack sheepishly looked around before chasing after his wife. He found Joann standing beside the couple's wagon with her head buried against Elizabeth. Both she and the baby were crying uncontrollably. Zack walked up and took Joann into his arms.

"I'm here. Everything is going to be fine," Zack soothed.

Joann sobbed too hard to speak. She kept her head buried next to Elizabeth's cheek and against Zack's chest. He didn't know what else to say so he stood there patting her back.

Abby managed to slip out of the church ahead of the crowd and made a beeline to her daughter. She managed to get Elizabeth into her arms and began comforting the baby. "Why don't you two head on home. Gideon and I will come shortly with Elizabeth. That'll free you from the baby and give you some time to feel better," she said.

Joann nodded her head, and Zack helped her into the wagon. They left the churchyard just as the coffin was being carried to the wagon.

The couple was nearly halfway home before Joann had gained a semblance of composure. She broke the uneasy silence by saying, "Seeing them put the lid on the coffin was too much. It brought back all those memories of seeing Tess for the last time. I still miss her so much." She started sobbing again.

"I know. I miss her, too, but God gave us Elizabeth. We need to be thankful for her," Zack replied.

"I know, and I am, but we're all going to die."

Zack turned his head and looked at Joann curiously. "That we are, but hopefully not for a long time."

"We've already lost Tess, and you nearly bled to death when those highwaymen shot you. Life is so precarious."

"But I didn't die. You can't go through life thinking that way."

Joann rubbed her hand across her mouth before confessing, "Death scares me so."

Zack pulled on the reins until the horses came to a stop, and turned toward his wife. "Joann, fearing death is not going to stop it from coming. The only thing that accomplishes is to make you miserable while you're still living. Life is for enjoying. We have each other and a beautiful baby girl. Let's count our blessing and enjoy each day. We have a good life these days."

Joann managed a smile before leaning her head against Zack. "I know, and I'll be fine. Funerals just bring back all the memories of Tess's death. And I am grateful for Elizabeth, but I don't want to ever think of her as a replacement. That wouldn't be fair to her. I just don't want to ever forget Tess. Let's get home."

"Sure, hon, but we'll never forget her. That I can promise you," Zack said. He tapped the reins to get the horses moving.

By the time the couple reached their cabin, Joann's demeanor had improved greatly. She managed to give Zack a warm smile as he helped her down from the wagon seat.

"While you put the buckboard up, I'll start lunch for my parents and us," Joann said.

"Do we have to feed Gideon?" Zack teased.

"You had better be nice to Daddy. He takes your side more than he does mine. If you're not careful, he's liable to figure out the lout you really are," Joann responded.

Zack gave his wife a wink as he turned to walk away.

Joann entered the cabin and began preparing the lunch. She had just finished frying the slices of pork when Gideon and Abby arrived with Elizabeth. The baby was sleeping so Abby carried her to her crib while Gideon took a seat near Zack.

As Abby came back from the bedroom, she asked, "Are you feeling better?"

"I am. The funeral brought back too many old memories. I'm fine now. It just dawned on me that I kept you from going to the burial. I'm sorry," Joann said.

Abby waved her hand through the air. "Don't worry about it. We paid our respects. Gideon is headed to town this afternoon and he can check on Finnie and Mary."

Wishing to change the subject, Gideon asked, "So how is the alfalfa looking this year, Zack?"

"Really good. The rain gods have been kind. It's the best crop I've raised yet," Zack answered.

Joann brought a plate of pork and another of bread to the table. "Everybody have a seat. I'm glad you asked about the alfalfa. Daddy, did you know that the Morris homestead right next to us is for sale? I think we should buy it. Zack doesn't."

Gideon scrunched an eye shut and pursed his lips. For some reason, Joann liked to drag him into mediating the couple's disagreements. For him, it was a no-win situation. Either he sided with one to the other's displeasure or he stayed out of it and drew the ire of both of them.

Before Gideon could speak, Zack said, "I still have so much land to clear on our homestead. I have my hands full with that, the alfalfa, and the cattle. I don't know what we'd do with more land. I certainly don't spend my time whittling on the front porch."

"We could get some more cattle for the Morris place," Joann suggested.

"I hadn't heard about it. When did they put it up for sale?" Gideon asked.

"Mr. Morris came by here last week and offered it to us," Joann said excitedly.

Gideon took a big breath and blew up his cheeks as he exhaled slowly. He glanced at Abby as he tried to decide whether to state his opinion. Abby showed no sign of getting involved and merely smiled back at him. "I'm not saying anything unless Zack says he wants my opinion, too."

Zack, looking as if he already dreaded what Gideon would say, nodded his head.

"All right, then. If you can afford it, I don't think you can ever go wrong by buying land. God isn't going to be creating any more of it and I think land values will keep going up. Even if you let it sit a few years, it'll be there when you're ready for it. And truth be told, you could add to your herd without really making much more work. I'm sure Ethan will buy the place if you don't."

"I already talked to Ethan about it. He told me to let him know when we make a decision," Zack said.

"Daddy took my side for a change," Joann gloated. "I knew I was right."

Zack grinned at his wife even though he was on the losing end of the disagreement. Seeing her back to her normal bratty self after such a rough morning was victory enough for him. Sometimes he wondered what about his wife had attracted him to her in the first place, but he surely did adore her. She certainly had a way of making life exciting. "Fine. We'll buy the land, but if we go broke, Gideon better never complain when we're living under his roof," he said with a bobble of his head at his father-in-law.

"I've already been taking care of you since the day I made the mistake of bringing you to Last Stand. Actually, I've been taking care of you since the moment I found you knocked silly on the trail," Gideon retorted.

Joann, reinvigorated from her triumph, did the biggest share of the talking during the meal, mostly about Elizabeth. Just as the women were cleaning up, the baby awoke. Gideon needed to get to town anyway, so he and Abby left as Joann prepared to feed the baby.

On the way home Gideon remarked, "Do you think Joann is all right? That was quite the change in mood."

"Oh, she's fine. The funeral just brought back all those memories of Tess dying. I think it says a lot with how quickly she got back to being herself. She's a strong girl now. She weathered the storm and lived to tell the tale," Abby said.

"I suppose so. We need to get home." Gideon popped the reins to speed up the horses.

When the couple got back to their home, Abby went to check on how Winnie had done babysitting Chance while Gideon quickly unhitched the wagon and retrieved his horse from the stall.

Gideon's previous horse, Buck, had meant the world to him. The horse had been his only companion in the years before he returned to Last Stand. After the horse had died a little over a year ago from taking a bullet during a gunfight, Gideon had been lost. He'd originally intended to catch a mustang to train, but nothing had ever come of the plan. Since then, he'd tried several horses, but none of them had met his satisfaction. He then had latched on the idea of contacting the Langley

Ranch in Fort Laramie, Wyoming. Gideon had worked there briefly in the summer of '78. The ranch had a magnificent stallion they called Leif that was half Quarter horse and half Arabian. They had crossed him with wild mustang mares. The first batch of foals had been born that spring. Gideon had left before ever seeing how the animals had turned out, but the offspring had looked promising. Caleb Gunnar, from the Langley Ranch, had written back and assured Gideon the breeding program had been a true success. He'd promised he would ship Gideon a fine three-year-old gelding. When Gideon received the horse a little over a month ago, he hadn't been disappointed with his purchase. The horse was a dark bay that looked a whole lot like his daddy and was well trained to boot. Gideon had named the animal Norse in honor of the stallion's Swedish name. The only thing left was for the two to trust each other fully. Gideon hadn't ridden Norse enough to know for sure he could count on him in any circumstance, and Norse had enough mustang in him that it would take time until he trusted Gideon completely.

"Good boy," Gideon said, patting the horse's neck. He saddled up and rode Norse at a walk until sure the horse's muscles were warm before putting him into a lope to town.

Finnie wasn't in the jail, so Gideon walked to the Last Chance. Delta was tending bar.

"Have you seen Finnie or Mary?" Gideon asked.

"Mary is in the back. I haven't seen Finnie since we all got back from the graveyard," Delta replied.

Gideon nodded his head and walked through the door leading to the back room. He found Mary sitting at the table sipping tea, seemingly lost in thought.

"Mary, are you all right?"

Mary twisted her head toward Gideon. "I wasn't expecting you. I thought Delta was coming for something. I guess I'm good."

Gideon took a seat adjacent to Mary. Where his relationship with Sarah was sisterly, his bond to Mary was far more complicated. There had been a time when the two had had feelings for each other before Abby had come back into the picture. They had remained close, however, and were lucky that Finnie and Abby were tolerant enough to allow the friendship to continue.

"We're going to find out who did this."

"I don't doubt that, but nothing is going to bring Charlotte back," Mary said before taking a sip of tea.

"We've certainly seen a lot of violence in our day," Gideon said with a sigh. He dropped his hat on the table and ran his hand through his hair.

"That we have. I hope I see no more, though I don't think that's very likely."

"What are you going to do about the café?"

"I think I'll let Juanita run it. The town has gotten used to the fact she's Mexican. That girl worked her butt off to win people over. Did you ever notice how people quit noticing someone's skin color after they start liking them? She's plenty smart enough. I'll just find me another waitress."

"That should work. I'll be glad when we get back to whatever the new normal is going to be with Charlotte gone. Finnie has been too quiet. Don't tell him I said so, but I find it annoying when he's not being annoying," Gideon said with a forced smile.

"Gideon, take care of him. I know he's hurting, and I don't want him doing something stupid when you catch the killer."

"Don't you worry about that." Gideon reached over and patted Mary's hand. "We're all going to get through this."

Chapter 6

The day after the funeral, Gideon warily climbed off his horse and walked toward the jail door. The previous evening, Finnie's spirit had been as low as Gideon had seen since the days when the Irishman fought the bottle. Gideon had every intention of being a supportive friend, but he certainly didn't relish the task. As he opened the door, he heard Finnie singing "Whiskey in the Jar" at the top of his lungs in his fine tenor voice.

"You're certainly in a good mood," Gideon yelled to get Finnie's attention.

Finnie stopped singing and turned toward the door. "Aye, I guess I am. I played with Sam and Cany this morning and realized how blessed I truly am. I'm not over mourning Charlotte by a long shot, but I just couldn't go there this morning. I needed to feel a little joy in my life."

"Good for you." Gideon took his seat and dropped his hat onto the desk.

"What are we going to do for fun today?"

"I don't know. I'm sure somebody will come up with something for us to do. Maybe Mary's reward will loosen up some tongues."

"I hope so. We sure don't have anything else to go on."

An hour later, the door to the jail flung open. A miner with dried dirt encrusted on his pants and boots came marching into the office. With each step, the hardened mud would break from the soles of his boots and litter the floor. "I want to report a robbery," the miner announced.

"Who are you?" Gideon asked, agitation in his voice at seeing the mess on the floor.

"Alvin Ledbetter."

"So, what's your story?"

"Last night, Landon Noble came by and told me he was giving up and heading home. Said he wasn't finding enough gold to have an aching back every night. He was sweet on that waitress that got herself killed – whatever her name was. With her dead, he didn't see any reason to stick around. This morning when I woke up, Landon and my rifle were both gone."

Finnie rolled his eyes. "Are you sure you didn't leave it leaning on a tree somewhere?" he asked skeptically.

Riled by the question, Alvin answered, "Of course not. I used it to shoot a rabbit last night and I go to sleep with it by my side."

"So, you think he snuck into your camp and took the rifle while you slept?" Gideon asked, doubt in his voice.

"I'm sure of it. Panning for gold all day makes for sound sleep. I never heard a thing."

"If I planned to come back to do a little robbing, I don't think I'd be mentioning I was leaving," Finnie said.

"I don't know why you two are giving me a hard time. I was the one that got robbed. I'm just telling you what happened. If Landon didn't steal my gun, well, somebody else sure did. And another thing that makes me think he's a thief is that he was wearing this little gold ring on his pinky finger. I'd never seen him wear it before. Looked like something a young girl would wear. I don't know why any self-respecting man would buy himself something like that."

Gideon and Finnie both sat up in their chairs and exchanged glances.

"How well did you know Landon?" Gideon asked.

"Oh, we shared a few meals together. He told me he hailed from Pueblo. That's about as far as it went."

"Do you know which hand he favors?"

Alvin pursed his lips and squinted his eyes as he thought about the question. "He's left-handed. I remember one time he was admiring my rifle and he sighted down it. He held it on the wrong side. Why?"

"Just curious. What kind of rifle was it?"

"A Winchester '73."

"What does Landon look like?"

"He's about twenty-five, medium height and weight, with mouse-brown hair. Nothing about him catches your eye."

"All right, Alvin. We'll try to find Landon and see if he has your gun. Check back in here in a couple of days," Gideon said. He stood and walked the prospector to the door to prevent him from lingering.

"What do you make of that?" Finnie asked as the door closed.

"Mighty suspicious, I would say."

"But why would this fellow kill Charlotte if he was sweet on her?"

"I don't think whoever killed her went in the café with those intentions. He had to use a kitchen knife to do it. That doesn't sound like a person planning on murder."

"All true but kicking in a door is a queer way to show a girl you're interested in her."

"Finnie, you know, I've about quit trying to figure out other people's minds. I have a hard enough time understanding my own on most days."

"So, I guess we're headed in the direction of Pueblo?"

"That we are. Let's take a packhorse just in case we have to go all the way there."

"Maybe we'll cross paths with Fred. We could kill two birds with one stone."

"I hope not. I really don't want to be the one to arrest him again. Let's get things gathered. I need to have somebody take a message to Abby. She'll be thrilled I'm sure," Gideon said sarcastically as he walked to the ammunition shelf.

Less than an hour later, Gideon and Finnie rode out of Last Stand. Getting to Pueblo was no easy task. The shortest and simplest route was to first go southeast past Alamosa and then eventually head north. Neither man was excited about the travel. They sat glumly in their saddles without talking.

Finnie finally broke the silence. "So, do you feel good about this?" he asked.

"Good as in how?"

"That this Landon fellow killed Charlotte."

"I've been mulling that over in my head. Everything sure points to him except I don't understand stealing the rifle. Why if you want to slip away unnoticed would you tell someone you're leaving and then steal his rifle? He should have had plenty of money from robbing the café to buy a gun once he made it to Alamosa without drawing any attention to himself."

"I thought the same thing. Doesn't sound like he's particularly intelligent, one way or the other. It's best not to try to understand the logic of a simpleton."

Gideon looked over and smiled at Finnie. "Good point." He pressed Norse into a lope.

The men made Alamosa in the afternoon and stopped in to see Sheriff White. The two sheriffs had worked together on previous crimes and had a good relationship. After getting the greetings out of the way, Gideon gave what little details he had of Landon Noble and asked the sheriff if he'd seen anybody matching that description.

"I'm afraid not," Sheriff White answered. "You know you're more than welcome to check around the saloons and hotels and whatnot. He could be here, and I not know it."

"Thank you, Sheriff. I think we will have a look around, but I doubt he stopped here. I'm not sure I'd recognize him anyway unless I saw the ring on his finger," Gideon said.

Gideon and Finnie walked to the Alamosa Hotel and went inside. An ancient little man stood behind the counter. His posture was so stooped over that he looked as if he were searching the ground for a dropped coin. He arched his head up to see who had entered the hotel, revealing glasses so strong that his eyes looked as big as a Great Gray Owl staring back.

As Gideon moved up to the counter, he figured he was wasting his time. He doubted the old man could tell the difference between a man and a woman let alone identify someone. "I'm the sheriff from Last Stand and this is my deputy. Sheriff White gave us permission to check around to try to find a man we're looking for," Gideon began before launching into Landon's description.

The old man braced his hands on the counter and forced his back straight. His eyes lit up and he began tapping his finger on the wooden top. "He checked in right around noon. I remember thinking I'd never seen a man wearing a ring like that. He got himself a bath and a shave. I think he's probably out getting himself supper now."

"Thank you, sir. You've been more than helpful. We may be back if we don't find him out and about," Gideon said.

"I'll keep my eye out for him," the old man promised.

Once they were outside of the hotel, Gideon said, "There's a lesson to learn. I assumed that old man would be useless. I sure was wrong. He was right sharp for his age."

"You thought that because you think you're smarter than everybody else," Finnie chided.

"I do not. I just didn't figure he could see well enough to notice anybody's features."

"Pff. You're like the pretty whore that thought she could get any man she wanted, and all the other girls would have to take seconds. She got showed up by the ugly whore that was real good at her job – if you know what I mean."

Gideon shook his head and loudly blew out his breath. "I concede that you must be smarter than me because half the time I don't even know what you're talking about. Let's go in that café over there," he said and pointed.

The men entered the café. The building was narrow and ran parallel to the street with just enough room for two rows of tables. As Gideon scanned the room, he noticed a man sitting alone that matched Landon's description. The suspect looked up nervously and made eye contact. He was trapped. His only path to escaping meant getting past Gideon and Finnie. As Gideon moved down the rows of tables, the man jumped up and ran toward the back. He hurled himself into the window, sending shards of glass raining down on the unsuspecting customers as he landed on the boardwalk. Landon Noble scurried out of view, leaving a trail of blood.

As Gideon and Finnie ran for the door, Gideon shouted, "I want him taken alive. That's the only way we're liable to know for sure if he killed Charlotte."

Landon climbed onto the first horse he came to and galloped away. The lawmen had to run a block to get to their horses. Out of breath, they hustled into the saddle and put their horses into a lope in pursuit.

"We'll just hold this pace and see if he runs his horse out," Gideon shouted.

"I know. I've done this a time or two," Finnie grumbled.

They followed Landon east out of town. The land was flat enough that they could keep the rider in sight.

"He's smart enough to slow his horse," Finnie called out.

"It doesn't matter. We didn't use up our horses today. He has to stop sometime," Gideon hollered back.

Landon continued on, holding his horse to an easy lope. After a few miles, he came upon a shallow, long gully. With a quick look over his shoulder, he rode his horse down the embankment and took cover along its edge. Gideon and Finnie pulled their horses to a stop well out of rifle range.

"Do you have a cannon handy?" Finnie quipped.

"You make an arc to the north and I'll go south. From here it looks as if that ravine is curvy enough that we can take some cover if need be," Gideon replied.

"What if he jumps back on his horse? Sunset is coming, and we've ridden our horses all day. We can't run them into the ground."

"I know that. His horse looked to be wearing down. It can't run much farther. We can push ours one more time if we have to. Remember, we need him alive. And make sure you don't shoot me while you're at it."

"Sometimes you're just plain insufferable. If I ever shoot you, believe me, it won't be no accident. It'll be because I finally got tired of your haughty ways." Finnie turned his horse off the road and headed north.

Still chuckling at his friend, Gideon headed south. The men made an arc far enough away to stay out of range and then descended into the gully. They tied their horses to scrub brush and retrieved their rifles before beginning the walk toward Landon. The snaky path of the gully allowed the men to dart from one side to the other with only brief moments of exposure. The first shot from Landon kicked up dirt and rock as Gideon ran to the other bank. As Gideon peeked around the embankment with his rifle ready, he saw Landon hustling toward his horse. Gideon fired three shots into the ground at Landon's feet, causing the young man to jump back for cover.

"Landon, you need to throw that rifle down and give yourself up or we're going to have to kill you. You can't escape," Gideon shouted.

Landon stepped into the open and fired in Gideon's direction. With the prospector in sight, Finnie brought his rifle up and fired. The shot sprayed Landon with gravel and he let out a yelp as he dove to the ground.

"All right. I'm going to throw my rifle down and put my hands up. Don't shoot me," Landon yelled.

The young man did as he said he would and stood with his hands quivering and blood running down his arm from the glass cut. With their revolvers drawn, Gideon and Finnie jogged toward him.

"I never thought you'd chase me clear to Alamosa for a damned old rifle," Landon lamented.

Finnie grabbed Landon by the wrist and yanked his arm down to see his hand. When he spotted the ring, he yelled, "You killed Charlotte." He pulled his arm back and decked Landon with a punch to the jaw.

As Finnie plopped down on Landon's stomach, ready to hit him again, Gideon ran up and tackled the Irishman. The collision sent both of them sprawling into the gully.

"Damn it, Finnie, stop it. We're not going to know a thing if you beat him to death. Now behave yourself," Gideon yelled.

Finnie got to his feet and kicked at the ground. "You should have let me soften him up a little," he hollered.

Landon held his jaw and moaned. Gideon walked over and stood over him.

"Where did you get that ring?" Gideon asked.

"I found it in the alley behind the café in Last Stand. I came to town Monday to sell some gold dust. I cut down that alley. The sun was reflecting off this ring just as pretty as you please. I picked it up and put it on my finger," Landon answered as he continued to rub his jaw.

Finnie took a step toward Landon, causing the young man to cower. "You better give me her necklace right now if you know what's good for you," he threatened.

"I don't know anything about a necklace – honest. You don't really think I killed Charlotte, do you? I was sweet on her and wouldn't have done her harm. I didn't even really steal that rifle. I played poker with Alvin one night and won it and then he reneged on me. Two other miners can back my story. I just figured it was mine."

"Then why did you jump through a window?" Gideon asked.

"Well, when I saw you, I knew what you were there for. It seemed like a good idea at the time."

"You've managed to make yourself look mighty guilty."

"I sure wish I never bothered with that rifle, but I still think it's mine."

"Empty your pockets."

Landon fished around in his pockets and produced twenty-one dollars in coins.

"Do you have any money on the horse you left in town?" Gideon asked.

"This is all the money I have in the world. I spent the rest on the hotel and a bath and a shave."

Finnie leaned in so his and Landon's face were inches apart. "I want that necklace back. I'm telling you for the last time that you'd better tell me where it's at."

"Mister, the only thing I'm guilty of is taking a rifle that rightfully should have been mine anyway."

"That and horse stealing," Gideon added.

"What are we going to do?" Finnie asked.

"Let's head back to Alamosa. He needs his arm sewed up and he can pay for the window he broke. I hope I can talk Sheriff White into not charging him with stealing the horse since we're returning it. That way, we can take him back home in the morning."

Finnie kicked at the dirt again. "I still think you should have let me get the truth out of him."

Chapter 7

A slow day at the doctor's office had caused Doc and Henry to move outside to a bench near the door. The two had passed the time shooting the breeze on nothing more urgent than the weather and fishing stories.

"Grandpa, I've been thinking about something. I know you've had a hard time finding another doctor to bring into your practice. What do you think about waiting until I graduate so that I can take the position?" Henry asked.

The question caught Doc totally off guard. Overcome with emotion by the proposal, he rubbed his chin as he contemplated an answer and steeled himself. The family had made jokes about Henry coming to Last Stand to practice with him, but no one had ever seriously discussed the idea. "Well, Henry, that idea warms my heart and flatters me. The thing is I don't know if I can keep working that long. Your grandpa ain't no spring chicken these days. I'm not sure you'd like living out here either. You've been in Last Stand enough to know this isn't Boston. You'd also be leaving behind a fine family."

"But you came from the East and made a life out here."

"That I did, but my situation was a little different. I knew I was never going to be allowed to marry your grandma or ever meet your daddy. I just wanted to get as far away as possible."

Doc had fathered Henry's father, John, while a student at Harvard. The family of Henry's grandmother were wealthy and had forbidden their daughter to ever see Doc again and had prevented him from ever seeing his son. A few years ago, John had showed up in Last Stand to finally meet his father. The following year, he had brought his whole family to meet Doc. A relationship had been forged that still caused Doc to marvel at the change they had brought to his life.

"But I've come to love this place. All the family does. Mother and Father could move out here when he retires."

"Last Stand does get into your blood. There are some fine people here. I'm not sure you'd ever meet the kind of girl you're used to back home though."

The comment brought a smile to Henry's face. "Mother isn't exactly like the other women in their circle of friends, and Father seems just fine with that. If I had women fussing over me like they do you, I sure wouldn't complain."

Doc let out a chuckle and slapped his leg. "That's because they know I'm old and harmless."

"Why didn't you ever marry?"

With a sigh, Doc rested his chin on his hand as he thought about the question. "I did keep company with women when I was younger, but I guess I never met one that could take the place of your grandmother. She was quite the girl back in the day."

Henry sat silently, lost in thought. Unaware of his actions, he started mimicking his grandfather by rubbing his chin. "Life sure can be funny. I spent all those years never even thinking about having a grandpa, and now, I can't imagine ever not having you in my life."

Doc threw his arm around his grandson. "Me either, Henry. Me either. I used to grouse about folks that sat around talking about their grandchildren all the time. I just didn't understand it. Now I'm the worst one of the lot. Let's revisit the subject of you moving here when you come back next year."

A few minutes later, Gideon and Finnie rode into town with their prisoner, Landon Noble. The lawmen looked glum, but Doc noticed that both of them relaxed their stiff postures as they rode toward him and Henry.

"I wish I had a job where I could just sit around and watch the people pass by," Finnie complained.

"Well, I could teach you how to read if you want to begin working your way toward college and medicine," Doc responded.

The insult caused Finnie to sit tall in the saddle. "I can read just fine, and you know it. That was a mean thing to say."

"Well, don't start what you can't finish then."

Ignoring the all too regular arguing, Gideon climbed down from his horse. "Doc, our prisoner jumped through a window and has fifteen stitches in his arm. After our ride, I figure you might want to clean the wound and treat it."

"Bring him in the office. What did he do?" Doc asked.

"He stole a rifle, and if D.A. Kile thinks there is enough evidence, he'll be charged with murdering Charlotte."

As Landon dismounted, he whined, "I swear to you that I never laid a hand on Charlotte. I've never harmed a person in my life."

"Let's go," Finnie said as he took Landon by the arm and led him toward the doctor's office.

Once inside, Doc instructed Henry to make up some soapy water. The doctor proceeded to rip the bandage away from Landon's arm, causing the prisoner to wince. As Henry mixed the soap and water, Doc examined Landon's face, neck, and both arms. He didn't say a word as he methodically did his work.

"All right, Henry. Get a cloth and clean the wound. Just dab at it. When you're done, repeat with clean water," Doc ordered.

Doc stood by patiently watching his grandson work. When Henry finished, Doc said, "Pat it dry and then douse it with carbolic acid. We're not going to bandage the wound. It could use some air."

"How does it look?" Gideon asked.

"It's fine. I don't have any concerns" Doc replied.

"Thanks, Doc. We'll get out of your hair and let you and Henry get back to holding down that bench," Gideon said with a wry smile.

"I might not be able to sit now. There are a couple of lawmen around here that are starting to give me hemorrhoids. Can Finnie take your prisoner to the jail? I want a word with you."

"Sure," Gideon said. He motioned for Finnie to go on with Landon.

After Finnie and Landon were gone, Doc said, "Are you sure you have the right man for Charlotte's murder? He doesn't have a scratch on him except for the window wound and a bruise on his jaw. I feel confident Charlotte clawed up her assailant."

"Finnie put the bruise on him. But to answer your question, no, I'm not sure. He was wearing Charlotte's ring and he hightailed it from Last Stand. That's all I'm sure of at the moment. He claims he found the ring in the alley. I'm not even sure he wasn't entitled to the rifle he took. I'm just going to hold him until we get things figured out."

"Well, all right. I just wanted to bring that up in case it hadn't occurred to you."

"Yeah, I noticed. I just don't want to let him get away until we know more. The D.A. may think there is enough to go to trial. We'll see. Unless there's something going on around town that I need to know about, I'm going home."

"Not to my knowledge," Doc replied.

"I think it's safe to say that there's no news then," Gideon said and winked.

Doc straightened his posture, looking like a rooster ready for a fight. "I don't know why I continue to consort with the likes of you and Finnie. The way you treat me in front of my grandson is reprehensible. I must be a glutton for punishment. But I'll tell you one thing – the next time you get hurt and I have to put you back together, I'm going to sew your asshole where your mouth used to be. It'd be a more natural look for you."

Gideon broke into such a fit of giggles that he got choked. He walked out of the office coughing and laughing so hard he barely could catch his breath. As he entered the jail, he still hadn't gained his composure.

"What in tarnation is wrong with you?" Finnie asked.

"I riled our fine doctor but good. He's getting more sensitive in his old age than a lovestruck schoolgirl," Gideon answered.

"Tell me about it. He plays rough these days, too."

"I'm headed home. You go on and get home to Mary and Sam. Just feed our prisoner later on."

"See you tomorrow."

"Have a good evening."

When Gideon walked outside, he saw Henry walking down the boardwalk.

"Where are you headed?" Gideon called out.

"Grandpa sent me on an errand down to the general store," Henry replied.

"Hey, Henry, I hope you know we just like to tease Doc. Finnie and I would both take a bullet for that man. He's saved my life more than once."

"Oh, I know. He would think you were mad at him if you didn't give him a hard time. He got you good today. Grandpa can certainly hold his own."

"Just wanted to make sure you understood. I'll be seeing you," Gideon said as he climbed up on Norse.

Anxious to get home to the family, Gideon forced himself to go at an easy pace. He didn't want to wear down the young horse. Chances were good that another trip would soon be in order to go see the Indian agent. While exhaling slowly, Gideon cleared his mind and stared at the mountains off in the distance. The sight of them always made him feel calm and his problems small. Sometimes, he even felt the presence of God in the majestic formations. As he neared home, he spotted Winnie walking back from school.

"How about a ride for the little lady?" Gideon called out.

Winnie startled at the sound of Gideon's voice and broke into a run for a couple of steps before realizing it was her stepdad. "You liked to have scared me to death. I still sometimes think about the time Benjamin got kidnapped going to school," she said as she marched back and held up her arm for Gideon to pull her up onto the horse.

"You were young. I would imagine that would leave a lasting impression. It did on me, too. I really didn't mean to scare you. Let's get home." Gideon nudged the horse into an easy lope.

"Thank goodness you weren't gone long. Momma is never as fun when you're away."

"Just remember that the next time you're mad at me. I'm the man that puts the smile on your momma's face," Gideon teased.

Abby and Chance were out in the garden. She looked up and smiled at the sight of Gideon and Winnie riding into the yard.

"Do you have room to take in a good-looking man?" Gideon hollered.

"I'll let you know when I see one," Abby retorted.

Gideon grinned and bobbled his head at his wife's comeback. He helped Winnie down and rode to the barn. After putting Norse away and feeding him, Gideon emerged from the building and scooped up Chance as the family walked toward the house.

"So, how was your trip?" Abby asked as they sat on the swing while the children went off to play.

"It was fine, but I don't want to talk about me. What did I miss?" Gideon asked.

Abby thought for a moment and then smiled. "Yesterday, I had Chance on the saddle with me as String and I checked the herd. Chance looked over at String and said, 'I'm a cowboy.' You know how backward String is and how serious these ranch hands are about the title of a cowboy. String gets this frown on his face and looks at Chance as if he's debating whether to correct our boy. I tell you it was comical."

"Thank goodness String knows cattle because he's pretty much awkward at everything else he does. He and Fancy have to make the oddest couple in the history of the world. Have you seen her lately?"

Fancy Broderick had been a prostitute that had agreed to testify against her former boss. To protect her, the decision was made to hide her at String's cabin. After the danger had passed, she and String had stayed together much to everyone's astonishment.

"She came by yesterday evening. I think she gets lonely out there by herself all day and needs a woman to talk to sometimes. We had a nice chat. She really is content out here. I guess after a life lived in a saloon, the peace and quiet of living with String seems pretty agreeable."

"I suppose. As fiery as that redhead is though, I'm still surprised she doesn't kill String. I've never been able to wrap my noggin around the notion those two are together," Gideon said, shaking his head at the thought of the mismatched couple.

"Well, they are. He's sure been good for us, and I've learned so much from him. This year's calves are looking good."

"Finnie and I are going to have to head out to see the Indian agent before long."

Abby leaned her head against Gideon's shoulder. "I know. I hate when we're apart."

"Me too. A certain daughter of yours told me you're not fun when I'm gone."

Abby made a snorting sound. "That's because she questions everything I tell her to do when you're not around. She's getting sassy. I miss my little girl."

"Winnie was always sassy."

"I know, but I used to be able to buffalo her with a stern look. That doesn't work anymore."

"Well, you have Elizabeth now. You'll be able to spoil her rotten and then send her home to Joann. That should be fun," Gideon said, smiling at the thought.

"That I will. I guess I'd better go start supper," Abby said as she stood. "A bath might put you in a most favorable light for later on this evening." She winked as she walked away.

Chapter 8

Gideon had just finished his second cup of coffee while Finnie and he discussed the plans for the day. Alvin Ledbetter interrupted the conversation when he walked into the jail. Something about the prospector's demeanor on his first visit had left a bad taste for the sheriff. Gideon tried not to grimace at the sight of the still dirty miner.

Not wasting time with a greeting, Alvin said, "I hear you brought Landon in yesterday."

"We did. He's locked up back there," Gideon replied, pointing his thumb behind him.

"Where's my rifle?"

"Your rifle is being kept for evidence. You can't have it."

"What am I supposed to do about a gun?"

"I hear they sell them at the gun shop. I have a question for you. Landon claims he won the gun in a poker game and you reneged. Is that true?"

"That's his word against mine," Alvin protested a little too vigorously.

"Landon gave us the names of a couple other men that were there. We'll see what they say."

"It ain't against the law to not pay your gambling debts."

Gideon leaned back in his chair and rubbed his scar. Alvin was really starting to get on his nerves. It took all his will not to go off on the miner. "I'm not so sure a judge will agree with that. It's kind of breaking a covenant."

"I'm not really sure what that word means, but I guess we'll let the judge decide then. Besides, I hear you charged him with murdering Charlotte. I want my reward," Alvin said. He placed his hands on the desk and leaned over, jutting his body far across it.

Gideon shot Finnie a look, knowing that either he or Doc had been talking in the saloon. "No, he has not been charged with murder and a reward will only be paid for information leading to a conviction. Now, get your face away from mine before I knock your teeth out and drag you into the street for a good stomping," he threatened.

As Alvin straightened his posture, he said, "You're mighty uppity if you ask me. You should be thanking me for leading you to Landon."

"Get out," Gideon yelled and acted as if he were ready to fly out of his chair.

Alvin nearly tripped over his own feet as he spun around and took off for the door.

Finnie glanced over at Gideon, figuring he best defend himself before all hell broke loose. "I never said we charged Landon with murder. I just told some folks we had arrested a man wearing Charlotte's ring and were trying to figure out how he got it."

Gideon shook his head. "You should have just kept quiet. We're liable to have a lynching if we're not careful. I've seen one and it's not pretty. Charlotte was well thought of and people are riled."

"You shouldn't have told Doc then. You know darn well he's the town crier."

The comment caused Gideon to chortle in spite of his irritation. "You got me there," he said.

"I guess I better go round up some breakfast for Landon."

"You do that, and I'll go see the D.A.," Gideon said as he picked up his hat and plopped it onto his head.

Gideon walked down the street and into D.A. Stephen Kile's office. The district attorney was a young man that dressed the part of his job with his tailor-fitted suits and neatly trimmed hair. He also made no bones about his future political ambitions. Gideon liked Kile and had always found him fair in the administration of the law, no matter the consequences.

"Sheriff, what brings you in here today?" the D.A. asked as he stood and offered his hand.

Gideon proceeded to tell the district attorney about Landon Noble.

When Gideon finished, Kile leaned back in his chair, laced his fingers together, and rested his chin on the back of his hands. "That's quite an interesting story you have there."

"So, is taking the rifle stealing or not?" Gideon asked.

"I'd say it falls in the gray area, but I doubt the judge would be pleased to have it brought into his court. I think we should hold him on the theft charges until you figure out whether he murdered Charlotte. We can always drop the charges just before the trial. That'll give you some time to work on things."

"Thank you, Stephen. I appreciate you working with me on this. I really don't know what to think. It looks bad for Landon by having the ring and disappearing, but he doesn't come off as a killer either. I just don't know."

"Sheriff, I trust you fully. You always do a fine job and I expect you will this time, too."

"Let's hope. I'll be seeing you."

The rest of the day was spent trying to confirm whether Landon had been in Last Stand on the night that Charlotte had died. The bartender at the Corner Saloon remembered the young man pining to him about Charlotte on that evening, and a bar patron also recollected seeing Landon there. Neither of the men could recall what time Landon had left the saloon.

Gideon and Finnie met back at the jail just before the sheriff planned to head home for the day.

"Are you ready for tomorrow?" Finnie asked.

"I guess I'll have to be. Last year's Fourth of July celebration went without trouble. I hope this year does, too. Of course, we didn't have all these darn prospectors running around here then. Let's hope we get to enjoy the day with our families and not spend our time separating a bunch of drunks."

"Mary has about worn herself out getting things ready. The extra beer just got here today. Cany has been a big help. He keeps Sam occupied so that Mrs. Penny has been able to help Mary instead of babysitting. Mary expects a big day."

"Speaking of Cany, I figure we should leave for the Indian agency on Sunday morning and take Cany with us. I'm sure his family is worried sick about him, and you and Mary are just going to get more attached to him the longer this goes on. If I had my druthers, I'd just send a telegram, but I hold out no hope in that getting us anywhere. Maybe we can find out the number of how many children are missing even if they might not all be around here. I'm going to put Zack in charge while we're gone."

Finnie let out a sigh. "I suppose you're right. Mary and I are going to miss that little boy. He's been a joy and he's even picked up a few words now."

"I'm sure you will miss him. Probably better to do this now rather than later then. It won't get any easier."

"I guess I already knew this since I had me an Indian squaw at one time, but I think I appreciate it more now that I'm older – we're all the same no matter our skin color."

"That we are, Finnie. That we are. I'm going home on that note. See you tomorrow."

∞

Gideon rode Norse to town like usual with the plan that Abby and the kids would come later by buckboard wagon for the annual picnic and fireworks. He and Finnie spent most of the morning helping build a makeshift stage for the entertainment and assisting the local businesses set up booths on the lawn of the courthouse.

By noon, the crowds started gathering on the lawn. Abby arrived and spread a blanket on the grass. Ethan and his family, and Zack and Joann with the baby, soon joined her and added their blankets upon the ground. Benjamin and Winnie began haranguing their mothers until they were allowed to go off and explore on their own. As some of the townsfolk began a comedy skit, Gideon and Finnie joined the families. Mary was busy serving beer at her stand, so Finnie was toting Sam and holding Cany's hand.

"Looks as if you have your hands full," Abby said to Finnie while attempting to burp Elizabeth.

"Aye, that I do, but I can think of a lot worse jobs than watching the little ones," Finnie replied.

"I couldn't agree more," Abby said just as Elizabeth let out a resounding belch.

Doc and Henry came walking up.

"Do you think you have enough food to feed a couple of Last Stand's finest bachelors?" Doc said as he lowered himself onto a blanket. "Some of you might have to help get me off this ground."

"Of course we do, for you," Sarah said in a flirtatious voice.

Abby leaned forward so she could see past Gideon. "So, Doc, whose fried chicken are you going to be eating?"

Sarah was considered one of the best cooks in the county. Abby begrudgingly accepted the fact, but she still enjoyed making Doc squirm and dance around the subject.

Doc beamed back a smile. "Why I intend to sample the offerings of all three of you fine ladies. I'd be hard pressed to find three finer cooks in all of the West."

While the others laughed and joked, Gideon made for poor conversation as he remained distracted with keeping an eye on the prospectors gathered near Mary's booth. "I sure hope those miners mind their manners. There's a heap of them. We're going to have a mess on our hands if they get rowdy," he said to no one in particular.

Ethan leaned back and braced himself with his arms. "Will you relax and enjoy yourself? The four of us would be pretty formidable against those boys if they get to acting up."

"That's choice coming from you. You quit being fun at about the same time I learned how to shave." Gideon's concern caused his voice to sound flat and without humor.

Ethan cut his eyes toward his friend and shook his head. Before he could respond, everyone was distracted by Chance gleefully sitting down next to Sylvia. The little boy had been infatuated with the six-year-old girl ever since she had first come to live with Ethan and Sarah.

Sylvia enjoyed the attention showered upon her by Chance. She threw her arm around him and gave him a hug. Sometimes, if she let her guard down, Chance would cause her a pang of sadness. He reminded her of her little brother that had died with her parents in a house fire nearly two years ago. She had only recently come to understand death and to remember bits and pieces of what happened on that horrible day.

"Looks like you have you a boyfriend," Finnie teased.

As Sylvia looked over at Finnie and smiled, she had a flash of memory of him bursting into her bedroom, his blackened face lit by a wall of flames.

"You're the one that saved me from the fire," Sylvia blurted out.

Finnie hated talking about that day. He and Sylvia had both nearly died as he tried to find his way out of the smoke-filled house. Afterward, Gideon and Doc had told him his actions were the bravest thing they had ever seen a man do. The town considered him a hero, and to this day, the mention of his deed still embarrassed him. "I was just the first one to get to the ladder. Anyone else would have gone up it if they had had the chance," he said.

Sylvia studied Finnie's face. She could see by the way that he barely could look at her that she had made him uncomfortable. Her young mind couldn't quite grasp why such a thing would be so. Another flashback came to her of Finnie carrying her through the inferno so hot that she had burn blisters on her arm and singed hair. At some visceral level, she understood Finnie was a brave man that had risked his own life to save hers. She maneuvered away from Chance and went to Finnie, leaning down and kissing his cheek.

"Thank you."

Finnie turned about three shades of red. He stammered out, "You're welcome, little lady."

Sarah, seeing Finnie's embarrassment, reached out and took her daughter's hand. "That was a nice thing you just did. Why don't you now go play with Chance, Sam, and Cany?"

Gideon managed to pry Elizabeth away from Abby. He nodded his head toward where Mary was busy passing out beers as fast as she could fill the glasses. "Mary is going to be making so much money that you'll quit being my deputy. She'll have you staying home raising Sam."

"He's a sight more enjoyable company than you've ever been. That's for darn sure. Of course, so is a rattler," Finnie said, relieved that Gideon had thrown him a line to change the subject.

The women began retrieving the food from their picnic baskets and setting it together for all to share. Once they finished, Ethan said the blessing. While the group ate, Mary managed to get away from her booth for a few minutes to join them for a quick bite. By the time Finnie managed to stuff himself with one last chicken leg, the musicians had taken the stage and some in the crowd began to dance.

As the afternoon wore on, the music became livelier and the crowd rowdier as more people arrived. Halfway through "Turkey in the Straw" the music abruptly stopped when an argument broke out.

Carter Mason stood glaring down at the much shorter miner, Alvin Ledbetter. The outburst came as a surprise to others standing nearby since Carter was considered levelheaded and was well liked in the community. He began twirling the end of his handlebar mustache in agitation. "I'm telling you for the last time to stay off my land. There are all kinds of public land around here. I suggest you stay on them," he yelled.

"I don't know what is public and private. Why do you care? I'm not bothering your cows," Alvin protested.

"I've worked hard to own my place and I didn't do it for you to come trespassing on me as you see fit. You stir up the silt, so my cattle can't get a drink of clean water."

"Ah, your poor cattle," Alvin yelled and swung his fist upward to deliver a blow to Carter's jaw.

A brawl ensued as prospectors and ranchers rushed to Carter and Alvin's defense. Gideon and Finnie took off in a run toward the fight with Ethan and Zack close behind.

"Break it up," Gideon yelled as he drew his Colt and fired it into the air.

Alvin, ignoring the warning, pulled a knife from the sheath on his belt and made a slash at Carter. The rancher jumped back, but not before the knife cut across his chest. As Carter let out a groan, his white shirt began to turn crimson. He looked down at the blood with a blank look on his face and brought his hands up to his chest.

Gideon came charging in and smashed his revolver down upon Alvin's head, sending the prospector crashing to the ground in an unconscious heap. "That's enough," he yelled.

Finnie, Ethan, and Zack stood beside Gideon with their guns trained at the prospectors.

Ten miners stood staring back at Gideon. None of the men had drawn their weapons, but most were resting their hands on the butt of their guns.

"I don't like your odds," one of the miners mouthed off.

Gideon took a deep breath and exhaled slowly. He said a silent prayer that there would be no gunfire. If there was, innocent people would surely get shot – maybe even his own family or people he loved. "At the moment one of you fires your gun, all of these ranchers here become deputies and are free to defend the law. That changes my odds considerably. You prospectors are nothing more than squatters. You don't pay taxes and you are not part of the community. If you boys don't start minding your manners, I swear to God I'll run every last one of you out of my county – your choice. Now, get the hell out of here."

The miner that had shot off his mouth continued to stare at Gideon, but three of the other men went to pick up Alvin to cart him off.

"We're taking Alvin to jail. You don't knife people in my town and get away with it," Gideon warned.

The three miners walked away, and the rest followed.

Carter began to get wobbly. A couple of ranchers took him by the arms to help steady him. With the danger having passed, Doc and Henry came forward to attend to the rancher.

"Walk him to my office," Doc commanded.

Gideon looked toward the stage. "Let's get 'Turkey in the Straw' going again," he called out to the musicians.

While Zack helped Gideon and Finnie drag Alvin to the jail, a couple of ranchers walked the unsteady Carter to the doctor's office. Once Doc had the rancher on the exam table, he and Henry scrubbed their hands. Doc then grabbed Carter's shirt and ripped it open, sending buttons bouncing across the floor. He began probing the depth of the foot-long cut across the chest with his fingers.

"You're going to be fine, Carter. You'll have a nice scar to show off when I'm done, but no permanent damage. I'm going to put you to sleep while we sew you up," Doc said.

"I don't want to go to sleep. I can hold still," Carter insisted.

"Are you sure?"

Carter nodded his head.

Doc turned to Henry. "I'm going to put a few stitches in the muscle where the cut is deepest. I want you to watch closely. Then I'm going to let you finish up while I guide you."

"Do you think I'm ready, Grandpa?"

"I know so. This is as good of a wound to start on as you can have. I might need you to sew me up one of these days and I just as soon you learn on Carter," Doc said and then winked at the rancher.

Chapter 9

Sunday morning found Gideon in an ill mood as he rode to town to meet up with Finnie before they began their journey to Ignacio to meet the Indian agent. Abby and the children hated when he left on trips, and he didn't cotton to the idea either. The goodbyes after breakfast had been a somber affair. Winnie, in one of her emotional states, had even cried. Adding further to Gideon's dour outlook was the fact that Zack had been less than thrilled to add the title of deputy to his list of jobs. To appease his son-in-law, Gideon had also deputized Blackie, the town's blacksmith, to help with the prisoners and watch over things. In spite of Gideon's mood, the thought of his interaction with Zack caused him to chuckle. When he had first brought Zack to Last Stand, the young man would have stood on his head to please Gideon. Those days were long gone – a sure sign Zack was indeed family.

Finnie's horse, a mount for Cany, and a packhorse were tied in front of the Ford home. Gideon walked toward the house, dreading what he would find. Mary answered the door, her eyes red with tears running down her cheeks.

"I'm sorry, Gideon. Seeing Cany go is hard, you know?" Mary said between sniffles.

Gideon gave her a hug.

"I know it is, but I'm sure he has a mother not sleeping at night as she worries about her boy," Gideon said.

"I know."

Finnie walked up to his wife and Gideon just as they separated. "I think Cany understands that we're leaving and where we're going. I signed it to him the best I could," he said.

"You make sure you take good care of him and that he's warm at night," Mary lectured. She rushed over to Cany, hugging him and kissing his forehead.

"Bye, Mary," Cany said.

Mary looked into Cany's eyes. Tears were welling up in them. "Bye, Cany. I love you."

Mary hoped Cany understood what she had told him. He stood there nodding his head.

"Love you," Cany said, surprising the others.

The boy turned toward Sam. In an imitation of Mary, he leaned down and kissed the toddler. "Bye, Sam. Love you."

Sam looked up at Cany and then toward his mother. His face contorted, and he started to cry. Mary had to pick up her son to comfort him. She managed to kiss Finnie goodbye and then darted out of the room, so she didn't have to see Cany go out the door.

Once outside, Finnie lifted Cany onto the horse. He and Gideon mounted up and the three somber figures headed down the street.

As they neared the edge of town, Finnie asked, "Do you think we're doing the right thing?"

"What do you mean?" Gideon asked.

"Mary and I would keep him in a heartbeat if it was best for him."

Gideon inhaled deeply and then blew up his cheeks as he exhaled. "I thought about that last night as I tried to go to sleep. Part of me kept thinking he'd be better off learning how to live in the white man's world. The other part kept saying he belongs with his people and his family. I guess taking him home is what won out."

"I hope we're right. I've been on that reservation and it's nothing to write home about. Those people have been stripped of everything they ever held dear. I fear there will be a day of reckoning for what we've done to the Indians."

"I know."

"Do you think we're doing Cany differently than we did Sylvia?"

When Sylvia had been orphaned, Gideon had learned she had family back in Pennsylvania that was not well thought of by Sylvia's deceased father. For the sake of the little girl, he made the decision to inform the family that the child had also died in the fire. Only Finnie and Doc knew his secret.

Gideon rubbed his scar before answering. "No, I don't. I couldn't care less that he's Indian. He's a fine boy. With Sylvia, we knew what we would be sending her back to. I would imagine Cany has a fine family. And I'm also not sure about fostering our culture onto him. I think he deserves to live in his own society."

Finnie had to turn his head and look away. "I sure hope you're right."

"Me too. Now let's get going. We have a ways to travel," Gideon said as he tapped Norse into a trot.

For the next two days, they journeyed at a steady pace, seeing very few travelers as they navigated the mountain trail toward Ignacio. After getting over the initial longings for home, Gideon and Finnie were enjoying themselves. Cany proved to be no trouble, and even though he understood almost nothing said, Finnie told the boy all the same stories that Gideon had heard at least a hundred times. The riding was peaceful with some magnificent mountains to stare at in the distance while daydreaming. Pine trees shaded a large part of the path and added some color. They stopped at noon to eat some jerky and hardtack before resuming their journey. About an hour later, Finnie spotted someone on foot up ahead.

"I wouldn't want to be on foot out here," Finnie remarked.

"I'm sure there's a story we're going to hear," Gideon muttered.

As they neared the man, he stopped and turned toward them to wait. He looked to be in his early twenties and stood tall and muscular as if he'd spent a lifetime working hard.

"You're out in the middle of nowhere to be on foot," Gideon said.

"A man came into my camp last night and stole my horse. I guess I'm lucky he didn't kill me. I see you're the law. Maybe you can catch him for me. By the way, I'm Chris Dowd."

Gideon noticed the young man wore a revolver and wondered if the story was true. "He didn't take your gun?" he asked.

"He got my rifle and saddlebags. He took my revolver and unloaded it, then tossed it to the side. I suppose he didn't want to leave me out here empty-handed."

Finnie stood in the saddle to stretch his legs. "What did this fellow look like?"

"He was short and wiry with dark hair from what I could tell by firelight. Didn't wear a hat and his clothes fit poorly like they weren't his. He pulled his gun from the waist of his pants and held it in his left hand."

Gideon and Finnie glanced at each other.

"Did he have a high nasal voice?" Gideon asked.

"Yeah, he did. Do you know him?"

"Maybe," Gideon answered. "You're free to ride with the boy until we get you somewhere."

Chris looked up at Cany, and a sour expression came over him. "I ain't riding with no Injun."

Finnie set his jaw. "What's the matter? Are you afraid his color will rub off on you?

"Nah, but everybody knows they roll around in shit so that deer and whatever else those heathens eat can't smell them coming. I got a whiff of him from here."

"You're mighty mouthy and ungrateful to the help being offered you," Finnie said.

"My pappy always said that you Irish were right next to Injuns in being the pig shit of the world."

The comment caused Finnie to climb off his horse and move toward Chris. "Maybe you'd want to back your mouth with your fist."

"Finnie, let it go," Gideon called out.

"Gideon, you stay out of this. You wouldn't let him disparage your German ancestry."

Chris laughed at Finnie. "How tall are you? Maybe five foot four? You might have shoulders like a bull, but a little runt like you can't even reach me."

Finnie raised his fist and began dancing in a circle around Chris. A confused look came over the young man. In all his years, he'd never fought any other way than standing toe-to-toe. He didn't know what to make of the Irishman's moves.

With Finnie's concentration focused on Chris's hands, he waited for the young man to make the first move. Chris threw a roundhouse that Finnie easily blocked with his left arm before lowering his hips and launching his whole body into a right hook that landed square on Chris's chin. The force of the blow sent Chris backpedaling and his arms flew to his sides. Finnie came charging like a mountain lion going for the kill. He delivered a left into the young man's stomach and then a right uppercut that sent him hurling into the air. Chris was unconscious as he landed on his back with a thud.

"I bet he thinks twice before he runs his mouth next time," Finnie said as he moved toward his horse.

In an annoyed tone, Gideon asked, "Do you feel better?"

"I do. Don't you get all high and mighty with me. I've seen you do worse. Just because I'm not the legendary Gideon Johann doesn't mean I wasn't right in what I did."

Gideon grinned and let out a snort. "You got me there. I have had my moments. Just for the record – I love the Irish."

Finnie burst out laughing. "You should. I'm just about the best thing that ever happened to you."

"Thank God you spared me one of your whore analogies anyway."

Cany's expression had not changed through the whole ordeal. As he had watched the events unfold, he had tried to understand what was happening. He had an inkling that the man had said something disrespectful about him and caused Finnie's anger. In his eyes, Finnie had proven to be a great warrior.

Finnie mounted his horse. "I guess we better get going. Chris Dowd can resume his walk when his head quits ringing."

"Try signing to Cany what happened so he doesn't think he's traveling with some madman."

Finnie began signing. Cany finally smiled as his suspicions were confirmed. He signed back to Finnie.

"He says I'm a great warrior," Finnie proudly boasted.

"Oh, Lord, that's just what that big noggin of yours needs floating around in it." Gideon nudged Norse into moving before Finnie could reply.

They had ridden a mile or so when Finnie said, "You know that had to be Fred that stole the horse."

"I know," Gideon replied quietly.

"His tracks are pretty plain to see. We could go track him."

"I'm not about to take a chance on getting Cany killed by dragging him along with us."

Finnie looked over at Gideon. "I don't think you would go after Fred one way or the other."

"We're out of our jurisdiction," Gideon said testily.

"It sure as hell never stopped us until now."

"You're right. I fully admit I feel torn about bringing Fred to justice. As long as he stays out of our county, I'm not going to worry about him. Doesn't the idea bother you? Finnie, he was one of us."

"Sure, it bothers me. I just have a bad feeling he's going to kill some innocent person before this is all said and done. He's already ridden with a gang that killed. They get like a dog after it gets its first taste of chicken blood."

Gideon nodded his head but didn't answer.

On the fourth day of traveling, they reached Ignacio just before sunset. Finnie and Cany set up camp along the Los Pinos river while Gideon rode into town. Ignacio wasn't much to see and couldn't really be called a town, just a few buildings thrown up together. Once Gideon had a quick look around the place, he managed to buy some boiled pork and cans of beans at a shack masking as a store. With his belly growling, he hurried back to camp. The food tasted as if it were a feast after days of hardtack, jerky, and some wild game. After the meal, they bathed in the river and turned in early.

In the morning, Gideon again left Finnie and Cany at the camp as he headed back to Ignacio. He rode to a building that obviously served as the Indian agency. Inside, Gideon found a clerk busily making entries into a ledger.

"May I help you?" the clerk asked.

"I'm Sheriff Gideon Johann from Last Stand and I would like a word with Mr. Bartholomew."

"Let me see what I can do," the clerk said. He opened the door to an office and disappeared inside the room.

Another man returned with the clerk. He looked to be in his forties with thinning hair, a bushy mustache, and barrel chest. His stroll toward Gideon suggested that of a man with confidence in himself and his position of authority.

"Mr. Johann, I'm Charles Bartholomew. It's good to meet you. I've been through Last Stand a time or two. Fine little town you have there. Come into my office," he said while offering his hand.

"Good to meet you," Gideon said, shaking hands with the agent.

After the men had taken seats in the office, Mr. Bartholomew asked, "How may I help you?"

"We found an Indian boy in Last Stand that we believe was stolen from the Southern Ute Reservation and sold. We think there may be more. I was hoping you might be able to shed some light on the subject."

Mr. Bartholomew straightened his posture and pulled his shoulders back. As he took a deep breath, his chest puffed up as if he were walling himself off from danger. "This is the first I've heard of such a thing and I would think I would know if it were true. I believe you must be mistaken as to where this child came from."

Gideon didn't appreciate the response he had gotten. He doubted Bartholomew was lying but figured he was defensive on being called out over something that had happened on his watch without his knowledge. "I don't think so."

"Where is this boy at now?"

"He's back in Last Stand," Gideon lied. "I didn't want to bring him all this way just in case I was wrong."

"Mr. Johann, I truly believe you are mistaken. I know some Indian agents don't have the best reputation, but I try to do right by these people. I think they would come to me if there were a problem."

"I don't suppose you would mind if I were to ride to the reservation and ask around then."

"I most certainly would," Bartholomew said as he braced his hands on the desk. "You have no jurisdiction there and I don't need you stirring up the Indians with this nonsense. I'm sorry you came all this way for nothing, but I can't help you. If I learn of a problem, I'll send someone for the boy."

"I'll not turn that child over to anyone but his parents. Don't waste your time," Gideon said as he stood.

"Good day, Mr. Johann. Show yourself out of my office."

With a scowl on his face, Gideon tipped his hat and left. He rode back to the camp where Finnie and Cany had packed everything away and were ready to ride.

"That didn't go well. We need to tiptoe onto the reservation," Gideon said.

"Well, I can do that. We'll just ride around Ignacio and go right there." Finnie helped Cany onto the horse before climbing onto his saddle.

A couple hours later, they arrived at the location where most of the Utes lived on the reservation. Tepees and a few one-room houses made up the camp. Their arrival caused a stir as Indians began to gather. Someone shouted out something that the only word Gideon and Finnie understood was 'Cany.' The announcement caused even more of the Ute's to come rushing out.

One of the Indian men stopped in front of the horses. "What are you doing with Cany?" he asked in surprisingly clear English.

Finnie decided it best that he did the talking since he'd dealt with the Ute tribe in the past. "We found him with a miner and believe he was stolen from here and sold. We are returning him."

A woman came rushing up and pulled Cany from the horse. She broke into loud sobs as she engulfed the boy in a hug.

"My English name is Simon. I believe you have been here before," the man said.

"Yes, I used to be with Raging River," Finnie said. At that moment, he spotted his former squaw. The sight of Raging River gave him a jolt he wasn't expecting after all this time. Back in the day, he had cared deeply for her. Seeing her again brought back a rush of feelings he didn't realize he even still had for her. He nodded his head toward her in a greeting.

Gideon climbed down from his horse. "Can we go somewhere and talk?"

Simon spoke to another man in their native tongue and then said, "Follow me."

Finnie dismounted and moved toward Cany. The young boy freed himself from his mother's embrace and faced Finnie. As Finnie knelt down and held out his arms, Cany walked into them and hugged the Irishman. Finnie wrapped his arms around the boy and patted his back.

"Cany, I hope you have a good life. I love you," Finnie said.

"Love you," Cany replied.

Finnie gave the boy a wink and then hustled after Gideon and the other two men so that he wouldn't break into tears. They were led into a small building and took seats at a table.

"We believe there were more children taken and we wanted a count to get an idea on how many we'll be looking for," Gideon said.

"Why do you care?"

"Why wouldn't I?"

The Indian smiled ever so slightly and nodded his head. "Six boys. It happened twice. Three boys each time. We reported what happened to Agent Bartholomew after the first boys went missing. He didn't want us off the reservation looking for them and promised to find the boys, but nothing came of it. After the second time, some of the men went looking for them off the reservation, but whoever did it knew how to disappear."

"I don't know if they're all around my town, but we aim to find the ones that are and bring them home," Gideon said.

"Thank you for returning Cany."

"We best be going. That agent forbade us from coming here. I didn't tell him we had the boy – I didn't trust him. And I guess for good reason. He lied about knowing about the kidnappings."

The two Indians extended their hands and shook with the lawmen before walking them to their horses.

"Do you want to tell Cany goodbye?" Gideon asked.

"No, once is enough. Let's go."

"I think we'll be back here anyway."

After they had ridden off the reservation and were headed toward home, Finnie said, "The older I get, the more I realize how funny life is."

"That is something we can definitely agree on."

"Who'd have ever thought a drunkard Irishman could now have a pretty young wife and a son and be missing a little Indian boy I only met a little while ago?"

Chapter 10

Sarah busied herself with polishing the kitchen table until the well-worn wood shined as well as could be expected considering its age. The piece had been handed down to her from her parents. When she and Ethan were buying furniture for the new house, he had wanted to replace the table with a new one, but she had held firm that they were keeping the one they had. Too many memories had transpired sitting around the old thing for her to ever swap it out for one that was shiny and new.

She sat down and started reminiscing back to the days of sitting at the table while feeding Benjamin as he sat in a highchair. The memory made her realize how young and naive she and Ethan had been back then as they had forged their way through parenthood. Her mind jumped to Sylvia's first tentative meals with the family when the traumatized child was scared and confused. No one could ever accuse Sylvia of being frightened now – she was proving to be quite the independent child these days.

Ethan came flying into the house and slammed the door shut. The abrupt entrance caused Sarah to startle and end her reverie.

"What's the matter?" Sarah asked with alarm in her voice. Ethan wasn't the type of man to act irrationally.

"That son of yours," Ethan replied, agitation in his voice.

"What's he done?"

"I sent him up in the loft to fork out hay into the corral while I was working on expanding the entrance to our old cabin, so we can use it as a shed. I noticed that no hay was coming out of the barn, so I climbed up into the loft and found him reading a book up there. I don't know what's gotten into him lately."

"You weren't too hard on him, were you?"

"I told him to get busy or I was going to toss him out for feed instead of hay."

The comment caused Sarah to smile at her husband. "Ethan," she playfully chided.

"He used to love to help me, and he was darn good help, too. Nowadays, he doesn't seem interested in any of it. He'd rather lie around and read. What's happened to him?"

"Ethan, he's thirteen now, and not a little boy any longer. His body and mind are going through changes and he's starting to get independent. We're about to embark on the dreaded teen years, but, honey, there are far worse things he could be doing besides reading a book."

"He loves those darn books more than he does this ranch. What if that never changes? I've worked so hard to grow this ranch so it's big enough for him to be a part of when he gets older."

"Benjamin has always loved books. That's nothing new. This just might be a phase he is going through, or it might not. It wouldn't be the worst thing in the world if he wanted to go off to college and be a lawyer or such. You just need to calm down. You're a good father, and I know when you think about it, you'll want him to do what makes him happy."

Ethan sat down at the table and began clicking his fingernails on its top. "I suppose, but it doesn't mean I like it. I always dreamed of Benjamin and me ranching together. I bet you're happy about all this."

"Ethan Oakes, if you know what's good for you, I suggest you don't go there with me. I just want Benjamin to do what makes him happy. Life is too short to do otherwise. I have to admit it does appeal to me to see him follow a profession that isn't dangerous. I've seen you and just about everybody else we know around here almost die from everything from bad bulls to outlaws."

"I bet I could bully Benjamin into being a rancher," Ethan said, his eyes twinkling.

"I'm sure you could. Maybe that should be your sermon for this week – how God wants us all to mold our children into what we want – come hell or high water."

Ethan started laughing. "God, I love you, and I don't know what I'd do without you."

"That's right, you don't, so you better stay on my good side so I stick around. Now let's talk about our real problem child."

"What has Sylvia done now and where is she?"

"She's out back playing if she hasn't wandered off. She hasn't done anything yet, but the day is still young. That is the most willful child I've ever seen in my life. There is no stopping her if she makes her mind up that she is going to do something. Benjamin used to wander off on his gold-seeking adventures, and God knows, he was the pokiest child ever in doing his chores, but otherwise, he always minded. She's a big believer in seeking forgiveness over permission," Sarah said with a sigh.

"Tear into her like you used to do Benjamin. You never had a problem setting him straight."

"I'm getting soft in my old age and I know it. And besides, I think of Sylvia as our own, but a part of me always remembers she's an orphan and has been through so much already in life. She's liable to grow up to be an outlaw."

"Well, don't expect me to do your job. She adores me."

"Sure, make me be the bad guy. Of course, I always was the one that had to make Benjamin mind, too. Nothing new there."

Ethan grinned at his wife. "It suits your personality a lot better than it does mine."

Sarah shook her head. "You're incorrigible."

"Seriously, I think the most important things are that Sylvia doesn't lie, isn't mean, and is extremely kindhearted. Those are way more important than the fact she's an independent little cuss. Joann and Winnie, as you like to say, are free spirits. Joann turned out just fine, and Winnie is well on her way to becoming a fine young lady, too. I think we're good."

"I sure hope so. She's liable to turn this hair of mine gray before it's all said and done."

"I certainly hope not. I'm getting a little too old to have to be finding me a new young wife," Ethan said. He reached for Sarah's arm and pulled her into his lap.

"You think you're so charming." Sarah kissed her husband.

"We might have time to slip back to the bedroom."

"I don't think so. Either one of them could wander in here at any minute. Nice try, but you're not that charming. There's always tonight though. Maybe that will provide you with something to take your mind off your book-reading son for the rest of the day."

∞

Abby and String spent the morning moving the herd to fresh grass. The cattle had been reluctant to leave their grazing ground, and the job of getting them all moving together with only two people to drive them had turned into an exhausting endeavor. When the herd finally reached the new pasture, Abby and String found that the little dam they had made in the creek to pool the water had washed out. They were forced to gather stones to repair the levee. It took a good hour, but they climbed out of the creek bed with the job done. Both of them were tired from their labors.

In the last year, Abby had started wearing men's trousers when she rode on the ranch. Dresses and riding britches just weren't practical for working in or riding through brush. The first time String had seen her in the pants, his eyes had about popped out of his head, and Abby thought he had even swallowed a little of his chewing tobacco, but as always, the cowboy kept his mouth shut. By the time they finished the repairs to the dam, the pants were soaked and muddy. They clung to Abby's skin and felt suffocating. She would have given anything to shuck them and ride home in her bloomers. Only the fear of String strangling on his tobacco kept her in them.

"I'm going home to get into some dry clothes. We've done enough for one day anyway. Go spend the afternoon with Fancy," Abby said.

"Yes, um," the laconic String replied.

Abby rode away feeling annoyed at her ranch hand. There were days where it would have been nice to converse with the man. Cattle were the only subject where String would actually become animated and carry on a decent conversation. As far as she was concerned, there was a lot more to life than just cattle.

By the time Abby made it home, the riding in wet pants was chaffing her thighs. She climbed off her horse and hobbled to the house. Winnie had been left to watch Chance with orders to wash the dishes and dust the furniture. Inside the home, Abby found Chance sitting on the floor playing with his toys while Winnie sat at the table making something out of papier-mâché. Flour for the glue was everywhere, including all over Winnie. A glance at the furniture and toward the kitchen revealed that none of the chores were completed.

"Gwendolyn Hanson, what is going on here? You've made a mess and not done a single thing I asked you to do. Sometimes I swear you are thirteen going on five," Abby hollered.

"I didn't think you would be back home so soon. After I finished this, I was going to clean up my mess and do my chores – honest," Winnie replied.

"How many times have I told you that we do our work first and then we play? Things need to get done around here. We can't just play all the time."

"You're so mean. The only reason you have me around is to do work. Otherwise, you would just send me off to live with Daddy."

"Winnie, I can't believe you said that. You know that's not true."

"I don't know anything except that you are not fun anymore. Maybe I should go live with Daddy."

"I'm sure that could be arranged if you wanted it."

"I bet you'd like that, but who would you get to do all the work around here?"

"Go to your room right now and don't you dare come out of there until I say so."

"I don't have to," Winnie said as she arose from her chair and struck a defiant pose.

Abby placed her hands on her hips and stared at her daughter. "You are getting too big for your britches, young lady. I'm going to count to three and if you are not in your room, you are going to be one sorry girl. One, two . . ." Winnie made a dash for her bedroom.

With the battle won, Abby glanced over at Winnie's project. Her daughter had been gluing paper onto a clay pot. Plastered on the side of the container were the neatly written words 'Momma's Flower Pot.' Abby dropped into a chair and stared at the gift Winnie had been making her. She felt like crawling under a rug and crying. Nothing had gone right today. She had chosen the wrong time to lay down the law with her daughter and to top it off, she missed Gideon terribly when he was gone.

Chance walked over to his mother. "Momma, are you sad?" he asked.

After a quick swipe of her sleeve across her eyes, Abby smiled at her son. "I'm fine. I don't like getting mad at Winnie is all." She leaned over and kissed Chance's forehead. "You go play now."

∞

Zack trudged into the cabin, his shirt and pants soaked in sweat. The first thing he spotted was Joann sitting in her rocker while breastfeeding Elizabeth. He gave her a little wave before heading straight to the kitchen and downing two glasses of water.

"Zachary Barlow, you are going to have a heatstroke one of these days if you don't learn to pace yourself. Quit trying to clear off the whole homestead in one day," Joann lectured.

After Zack plopped down into a chair at the kitchen table, he said, "I know. I catch myself going at it as if I'm trying to put out a fire. I do it without even thinking. And now I need to clean up and get to town. I'll sure be glad when Gideon and Finnie get back."

Joann put Elizabeth over her shoulder and began patting the baby's back. "Well, stop it. We don't need you sick."

"While I was working, Mr. Morris came by to check if we wanted the land before he listed it in the paper."

"What did you say?"

"I told him to come talk to you since you're the boss."

"Zack," Joann chided.

"We're the new owners of the Morris homestead."

Joann let out a squeal that caused Elizabeth to bobble her head. "I know we're doing the right thing. You'll be glad we did this when you look back on it one of these days."

"I'll remember that when I'm out there working myself to death while you're sitting in your rocking chair passing the time," Zack said and took another long swig of water.

"I helped you a lot until I got pregnant – and that's your fault. I always told you that playing with a hot oven will get you burned."

Zack let out a snort. "Most ovens are content to stay in the kitchen. You're the first one that ever chased me or ran so hot."

"Well, fine then. That can be arranged. I sure never heard you complain before now."

"I wasn't complaining. My point was I don't think I should get all the credit for making our daughter."

"Get over here and look at her. I want to know who you think she looks like." Joann cradled Elizabeth in her arms for a better view.

Zack slowly got up from the chair and walked toward Joann and the baby. His eyes happened to fall upon the floor below the rocker. Sometimes the sight still gave him a jolt. The boards were worn smooth and shiny from when Joann had spent hours on end rocking after Tess died. She had been so devastated by the loss that she barely functioned, and there had been days when he had thought he would never have his wife back in any meaningful way. Those had been some bad times. Not wanting to think about the past, he quickly looked up at Joann's smiling face.

"With those blue eyes, you already know she looks like you," Zack said.

"There's more to her than just her eyes. What about her features?"

"I don't know. I think all babies look the same for the most part. I'm sure she'll look like your side of the family. Your bunch doesn't like to share anything, and I'm sure that includes what Elizabeth looks like."

"You big baby. You know my family adores you. Daddy would have run you out of Last Stand before you ever got the chance to marry me if he didn't think you were the one. I bet we have a boy someday that looks just like you."

"We'll see."

"Elizabeth is almost asleep. I tell you what – we'll go down to the waterhole and I'll scrub your back for you before you head to town." Joann gave him a wink.

"What will we do with the baby?"

"We can put her in her basket and take her with us. It's not like we're going to let the big bad wolf sneak up and get her."

Zack grinned. "So, you are still chasing me then."

"Let's just say that seeing Poppa all sweaty has got Momma's oven running a little hot today."

Chapter 11

The return trip from the reservation had made for dull travel for Gideon and Finnie to the point of being unusually quiet considering the Irishman's love of gab. During the entire journey, they hadn't so much as encountered a rainstorm or a cold night. Most of their time had been spent riding in silence while staring off at the still snowcapped mountains.

About an hour out from reaching Last Stand, Finnie said, "It'll sure be good to get home and see Mary and Sam. I've sure missed them. I'm missing Cany, too. Funny how you can get attached to somebody so quickly."

"I know you miss him. And you're right about sometimes having an instant bond with another person. I also believe that bond can last a lifetime whether you ever see each other again, too."

"That's just a fancy way of saying I'll always miss him."

"Maybe. During all those years I was away from Last Stand, I had trained my mind not to think about things back home, but I never forgot about Abby or Ethan."

"I notice you didn't mention me."

Gideon looked over at Finnie and grinned. He knew his friend was mostly joking, but there remained a part of Finnie that always needed to hear he was considered a good friend. "I did think about you sometimes and wondered whatever happened to you. And for the record, I searched you out as soon as I knew where you were."

"So you say."

"You should have named Sam after me instead of Doc. You wouldn't have ever known Mary existed if I hadn't dragged you kicking and screaming all the way to Last Stand."

Finnie snorted. "You do have a point, but Mary and I both agreed that the world couldn't stand two Gideons. You are sure right about me being bad company when you brought me from Animas City. I'm surprised Zack or you didn't knock me in the head and leave me by the side of the road."

Gideon grinned and shook his head but didn't reply.

"Seeing Raging River again at the reservation was kind of a shock. I didn't think I'd feel anything, but I was wrong. Mary is the love of my life, but I guess Raging River will always have a place in my heart," Finnie said.

"Kind of goes back to what I already said about bonds lasting a lifetime."

"I suppose."

"I'm sure glad nobody can hear this conversation. We sound like a couple of girls talking about this stuff. If you get any more sensitive, you're liable to want to hold hands with me or something."

"Gideon Johann, you're like the whore that the old boy visited one too many times. Sometimes the goody just plain gets all gone."

A short time later, the two men arrived in Last Stand and rode straight to the jail. They found Zack coming out of the cell room with the prisoners' empty supper plates.

"It's about time you two returned. I was beginning to think the Indians got you and I'd be forced into being sheriff," Zack grumbled.

"Good to see you, too, Zack," Gideon said. "It would be a shame if my daughter became a widow with a new baby and all."

Zack grinned at his father-in-law. "So you say."

"I notice a bruise on your chin and you're carrying three plates. What happened?" Gideon asked.

"One of those darn miners got into it with a cowboy. When I went to arrest him, a bunch of the other prospectors surrounded him. I thought I was going to have trouble on my hands, but I backed them down. Then, when I walked him to the jail, he sucker punched me."

"I hope you laid him out," Finnie interjected.

"Nah, I just shoved him down to the ground and then kept my eye on him."

"You should have wiped the floor up with him. You can't let anybody get by with disrespecting you," Gideon said.

"I know, but I didn't want to start a riot with me being here by myself. All those miners followed us outside and were watching."

"Those miners are going to think they run this town if we're not careful," Finnie warned.

"That will be a cold day in Hell," Gideon said. "They have about pushed me to my limit."

"Let's talk about something else. How are you guys?" Zack asked.

Finnie dropped into a chair. "I'm as tired as a coonhound after an all-night hunt."

"You kind of smell like one, too," Zack offered up.

Gideon glanced down at Finnie. "It's getting harder and harder to remember when Zack was a quiet young man trying to win our approval. That's what happens when they become family."

"We're both to blame. You should have never let him around Joann, and I shouldn't have taught him how to box. I couldn't help but take pity on him after we got in that scrape in Animas City and he used his face to stop punches. A few more fights like that and he wouldn't be so pretty or cocky. No woman would have wanted him."

Zack unfastened his badge and dropped it onto the desk. "You two are getting delicate in your old age, but, nonetheless, I'm glad to have you back."

"How are Joann and Elizabeth?" Gideon asked.

"They're good. Elizabeth almost slept through the night. It felt like Christmas."

"Thanks for helping out. Get on home and give my girls a kiss."

After Zack had left, Finnie asked, "What are we going to do for fun tomorrow?"

"It's time we start rounding up the Indian boys."

"Aren't we going to arrest the miners for buying the boys? We let that old codger go."

"We should, but I don't think so unless they've mistreated the boys. We might get more cooperation that way and not stir them up any more than they already are."

"Sounds about right. Well, I've seen enough of you for a while. I'm going to go find Mary and Sam."

"I'm right behind you. You can come in late in the morning. We need our beauty sleep. See you tomorrow."

Finnie dropped his horse off at the livery stable and then walked home. He found Mary feeding Sam before she left to go to the Last Chance. Mrs. Penny was reading her Bible in her room while she waited for Mary to leave before she began babysitting. When Mary saw Finnie come through the doorway, she dropped Sam's spoon and ran to her husband, throwing her arms around him.

"I'm so glad you're home. Things are just not the same when you're gone. God, I missed you," Mary said.

"I missed you, too. You might not want to squeeze me so. I'm a little smelly," Finnie said.

Mary broke into a giggle. "I don't care. It might keep the cowboys from pestering me tonight."

Sam started swinging his arms in excitement at seeing his father. "Daddy. Daddy," he called out.

Finnie broke from Mary and picked up Sam. He kissed the little boy's cheek. "Hello, little man," he said and hugged Mary again.

"Did you find Cany's family?"

"We did. He's home. How are you feeling about things?"

"I'm fine really. Of course, I'm missing him, but me being an orphan gives me some perspective. Cany would have had us if he stayed, but I know what it's like to wonder about where your parents are. I wouldn't want that for him. He's where he should be."

Finnie made a sad smile. "You are special, you know that?"

"I doubt that, but it's sweet, nonetheless. I wish I could stay, but Last Chance is calling. I'll see you when I get home."

"After I take a bath and play with Sam, I'll come down to the saloon to have a beer after he falls to sleep."

"Good. See you later." Mary gave kisses to Finnie and Sam. She glanced at the clock and then darted out the door.

"Daddy is going to take a bath and then we can play," Finnie said as he walked to the sink and began pumping water.

∞

Gideon arrived home just after his family had finished supper. Once the greetings were out of the way and he'd put Norse in the barn, he followed Abby into the house and took a seat while she started heating water for him to take a bath. Winnie disappeared into her room with Chance following her.

As Gideon dropped his hat onto the table, he said, "Something doesn't feel right. What's wrong?"

"Winnie is still mad at me." Abby took a seat across from Gideon and explained the incident with the papier-mâché.

"She'll get over it. I don't know why you're making such a big thing out of it."

"I know she will, but I really hurt her feelings. String and I had had a bad morning and I returned in an ill mood. I was in the right, but it was one of those times where I should have just let it slide. If I had noticed she was making something for me I would have. I feel terrible about it. I've apologized for being so harsh, but you know Winnie. She's a sulker."

"You've been doing this parenting thing a lot longer than me. This can't be your first mistake. It's not like you beat her for something she didn't do."

Abby smiled at her husband. "No, I've never beaten her. It's just that she's a young lady now and so sensitive. She's going through a lot of changes. I can remember what that feels like. Part of the time you still feel like a child wanting to be pampered, and part of the time you think you're an adult that should be able to do what you please."

Gideon reached across the table and took Abby's hand. "Trust me, I've been around Winnie enough years to know it would take a lot more than this to keep her down. She'll be back to normal in another day or two, and by the day after that, you'll be ready to kill her again."

Abby let out a giggle. "You're probably right. So, tell me about the trip. You were obviously too busy to find time for a bath."

Chapter 12

Bright sunlight shining through the window jarred Gideon awake. He reached for Abby and found her not in bed. After quickly dressing, Gideon rushed downstairs to find that Abby had already fed the children and sent them outside so as not to wake him. He groused at his wife for letting him sleep so late as he headed to retrieve his gun belt. Before he made it halfway across the room, Abby adamantly ordered him to take a seat while she fixed them breakfast. She left no doubt that his job could wait while they enjoyed one meal together before he traipsed off to town. With the realization the battle was already lost, Gideon grinned and sat down at the table while Abby cooked. He didn't even bother to rush in eating his eggs, biscuits, and bacon while he listened to his wife talk about the cattle herd.

After finally telling his family goodbye and saddling Norse, Gideon pointed the horse toward town. The extra sleep had done wonders for how he felt. He could almost pretend he wasn't forty-two years old as long as he ignored the fact that he had needed the extra rest. Norse didn't seem to be worn down at all from the long trip, so Gideon put the gelding into a lope to make up some lost time. As he locked into the rhythm of the animal's stride, he tried to imagine what grief Finnie would throw his way for getting to town so late. Gideon arrived in Last Stand to find Finnie coming out of the stable with his horse in tow.

"You didn't get around any faster than I did," Gideon said.

"Aye, I fear it is so, but I do have some kick in my step. That bed felt wonderful," Finnie replied.

"I hear you. That ground gets harder every year. Let's head to the north channel of the river. I think that's where a lot of the prospectors are panning."

Finnie climbed into the saddle. "I may feel good, but my arse could sure use another day away from a horse's back."

"I'm going to try to get that image out of my mind." Gideon nudged Norse into a walk.

They headed northwest out of town and rode for nearly an hour before they encountered the first prospector panning along the river.

"Hey, we're looking for any prospectors that have Indian boys with them. Do you know of any?" Gideon asked from atop his horse.

The miner looked up suspiciously at the two lawmen. He stammered a moment and asked, "Why do you want to know?"

Gideon had begun to get his fill of the miners and was in no mood to dally with them. "That is none of your concern. Now answer the question or I'll lock you up. You obviously know of someone."

"Lock me up for what? You can't do that."

"I don't have to have a reason today," Gideon said, swinging his leg over his horse to dismount.

Just as Gideon's foot touched the ground, the miner hollered, "All right, all right, I'll tell you. Follow the river another half mile and you'll find Dexter Horner. He's got a boy. You'd better watch him though. He's a mean one."

"Thank you. Now that wasn't so hard, was it?" Gideon then climbed back onto his horse.

As they rode away, Finnie said, "Maybe we better proceed cautiously and surprise this Dexter fellow."

"I don't think he's going to just start shooting at the sight of the law riding up to him. We're liable to scare the boy if we sneak up on them. We'll be fine," Gideon assured him.

The men continued following the river, passing two other prospectors as they rode. Up ahead they spotted a large man and boy panning in the stream. The prospector saw them, too. He grabbed the boy around the waist and took off running with the child tucked under his arm, scooping up his rifle as he headed for a tree line.

Gideon and Finnie spurred their horses into the nearest woods and took cover behind a couple of cottonwoods. A narrow clearing separated them from the timber where the prospector and boy had taken refuge.

While peeking around the tree, Finnie said, "I guess he heard about us taking Cany from that old codger. One of these days you're going to learn to listen to me once in a while."

"Yes, you were right, and I was wrong. Does that make you feel better? Figure out how we can resolve this without shooting at the miner, so we don't endanger the boy. I promise I will listen."

"Oh, sure, you are all ears now that we're in a pickle. You are the confoundest man I've ever known."

"I don't believe confoundest is a real word."

"Remind me to contact Webster when we get back to get the word added to the dictionary with a picture of you beside it," Finnie growled.

A shot rang out, cutting through the leaves above them.

"Webster is dead."

"He's liable not to be the only one before this day is through. I wish we could see them. This Dexter fellow probably has a horse up there and could ride off without us seeing them go."

"He's likely planning to hold us off until dark then leave, or he would have already skedaddled. You stay here and shoot up high to not hit them but keep his attention. I'll work my way through the woods and try to surprise him," Gideon said.

"No, I'll go. You might not be able to use a gun on him. That fellow looked big. He'd beat you like a drum."

"I'm good with my fists and you know it, and I'm taller than you," Gideon said defensively.

"All true, but I probably have forty pounds on you and you know that, too. And unless he's a trained boxer, there's no way he can whip me. You haven't seen that happen yet and I doubt you ever will," Finnie said. He took off through the trees so that he could avoid any further argument.

"That hardheaded Irishman," Gideon muttered to himself. He raised his rifle and fired a round high into the trees toward the miner.

Finnie worked his way through the woods toward where the clearing ended in a line of trees he could use for cover to cross over to the area where the miner hid. The tree line was a good distance away and his shirt became drenched in sweat as he jogged. He began to pant from the exertion and would have stopped to catch his breath if time would have allowed. "I'm getting too old for this stuff. I should just be a bartender for Mary," he mumbled.

The occasional crack of gunfire reached Finnie, giving him an incentive to keep moving. He made it to the tree line and worked his way across to the woods where Dexter Horner hid. The ground sloped uphill and he labored to the top before descending the back side to make his way toward the prospector for a surprise attack from the rear. As Finnie maneuvered toward the sound of the gunfire, he finally caught sight of the miner and the boy. He stopped and leaned his back against a tree as he sucked in deep breaths of air in hopes of getting back his wind. After pulling his hat off his head, Finnie mopped his brow with his sleeve to stifle the sweat running into his burning eyes. A shot fired by the miner caused Finnie to jump and peek around the tree. The miner and the boy were too preoccupied with Gideon to notice him.

Once Finnie had decided that his best option was to charge Dexter and club him with his rifle, he whispered to himself, "I hope this works." He grabbed his Winchester by the barrel and hoisted it above his head before charging.

The Indian boy heard Finnie trampling across the noisy forest floor. He let out a yelp of surprise, causing the miner to spin around to see what the commotion was. Finnie watched in dread as the man brought his rifle up to his shoulder. The deputy knew he was as good as dead if he didn't react quickly. With no time to get his Winchester in position to shoot, Finnie hurled the weapon as hard as he could toward Dexter. The gun smashed into the miner's raised left arm and then caught his chin, knocking his rifle askew as it fired. Taking advantage of the situation, Finnie began pummeling Dexter's face to the point the miner dropped his rifle to defend himself. From the corner of his eye, Finnie saw the boy take flight.

"Gideon, the boy is running. Get him," Finnie bellowed before throwing another punch.

Much to Finnie's surprise, Dexter continued to stand like an old oak weathering a fierce storm. The miner could certainly take a punch. He reared his arm back and delivered a sweeping right hook that landed on Finnie's chin. The force of the blow drove Finnie backward, and as he sought to regain his balance, Dexter charged like a mad bull. Before the prospector crashed into his chest, Finnie managed to get his arms up to avoid having them pinned to his sides. As he fell, he managed to throw Dexter to the side so the miner wouldn't land on him. Finnie hit the ground hard with a thud. The force of the landing dazed him, but he remained cognizant enough to know that if he didn't get up, he would be pinned to the ground and beaten to death. Willing himself to move, Finnie struggled to get off the ground. He saw Dexter doing the same a few feet away. Dexter reached for his revolver. Finnie drew his Colt and fired at almost point-blank range. The shot hit the prospector in the chest and launched him backward, but Dexter never stopped trying to retrieve his pistol. Finnie fired twice more into the prospector to ensure he never drew his gun. Even in dying, Dexter fell to earth like an old tree begrudgingly giving way. He hit the ground and did not stir. After Finnie holstered his weapon, he dropped onto his butt. He didn't have the strength to move.

Gideon had taken off for the clearing after hearing Finnie holler. He stood there searching for any sign of movement. The Indian boy came sprinting out of the woods about fifty yards from him. He took off along the riverbank headed away from the sheriff.

"We're here to help you," Gideon shouted.

The boy looked over his shoulder but kept running. Gideon took off in a dash, cursing under his breath as he negotiated the rocky riverbank in boots. Much to his relief, he soon realized he was much faster than the young boy was. His long strides gained rapidly on the child and he swooped in, grabbing the boy by the collar. The boy twisted around frantically and tried to kick his captor. Each time he swung his leg, Gideon would jerk the child's shirt and throw him off-balance, so the blow would go astray. With kicking failing to work, the boy sunk his teeth into Gideon's wrist.

"Damn it to hell," Gideon yelled as he slung the child facedown to the ground. He hopped onto the boy's legs and pinned his body so that he was helpless. With the boy subdued, Gideon inhaled deep breaths to try to get some air into his lungs. Blood trickled from his wrist onto the boys back.

Finnie finally sauntered along the river toward them. "I see you caught him."

"We have us a little Crazy Horse. He took a chunk out of my wrist. Cany he is not. Where's the miner?" Gideon asked.

"I had to kill him."

"What happened to all those boxing skills you like to brag about?"

"I just about bit off more than I could chew. That miner proved stronger than an ox. He went for his gun is the only reason I shot him though."

"I guess we will be more careful the next time we go to retrieve a boy."

"I think that was my idea in the first place."

"I'm going to attempt to hold this wild Indian without getting kicked or bit. You sign to him that we are going to take him back to his people." Gideon grabbed the boy by each shoulder and lifted him off the ground. He held the child at arm's length while facing him toward Finnie.

Finnie began signing. When he finished, he said, "I did what you said and also told him we wished him no harm. At least, I think I did. I'm really not very good at this."

"I'm going to let him go and we'll see what happens." Gideon released the boy.

The boy spun around and gave Gideon a ferocious look but made no attempt to escape. He then turned toward Finnie and signed.

"He told me he would come with us," Finnie said.

"That's a start, I guess. I don't know what we're going to do with him until we return him to the reservation. We really need somebody that can speak the language. Let's go retrieve the body and get back to town. I think one rescue is enough for this day."

"We are going to have the miners riled more than ever now."

"Just let them cause trouble. I've had about all of them I care to see in this lifetime."

Chapter 13

The Indian boy showed no emotion when Gideon and Finnie led him to the miner's body. He didn't bother averting his eyes either but stared at the corpse as if maybe he might be begrudgingly impressed that Finnie had felled the massive man. The lawmen had a heck of a time getting the prospector across the saddle of his horse. They strained, grunted, and groaned until the task was finally completed. After returning to their horses, Gideon mounted up and held out his arm for the boy. The boy looked at him warily but allowed Gideon to pull him up onto the saddle. With the child in place, they headed toward town. Along the trail by the river, the prospectors would pause in their panning for gold, and give cold, hard stares before resuming their work.

Once they reached Last Stand, they dropped the body off with the undertaker without drawing much attention to themselves. Only a few folks on the boardwalks noticed and stopped to gawk.

Gideon paused as they walked out of the undertaker's office. "You go ahead and take the boy to the jail. I have an idea on somebody that could watch him. It wouldn't be fair to Mary to watch another child. She has her hands full with her businesses, Sam, and grieving the loss of Charlotte – and taking care of you for that matter. Plus, she doesn't need to keep getting attached to boys that will soon be gone. And besides that, I don't trust this boy like I did Cany. Me, you, and Ethan all have children small enough that he could hurt them if he took a notion to do such a thing."

Before speaking, Finnie rubbed his chin. His jaw pained him with a dull ache and was beginning to get stiff from the blow the miner had landed. "I'm in no mood to argue with you. Whatever you think, is fine with me."

Gideon did a double take at his friend, having expected guff. He contemplated saying something pithy then thought better of it. "I'll see you soon."

After a short trip down the street, Gideon walked up onto the veranda of Pastor Roberts home and knocked on the door.

The Methodist preacher answered the door and greeted Gideon with the same joke he always used. "Gideon, have you come to cross over to the winning side and leave behind Ethan's church?"

"I would if it wasn't for Abby. She has a thing for big blond men," Gideon replied with a smile.

"What can I do for you?"

Gideon explained the situation with the Indian boy, then added, "To be honest with you, I don't really trust this one around small children. I thought of you since your kids are all grown, but I wanted you to be aware that he could be a handful."

"I appreciate your honesty. I'd be honored to watch over him as long as you need."

"Don't you think you should talk to Cassie first?"

The pastor smiled and reached out, putting his hand on Gideon's shoulder. "Don't tell my wife I said so, but when you've been married as long as we have, I know exactly what she would say. She loves children, even brown ones that won't understand a word she says. She'll be delighted to have him."

"Thank you. I surely do appreciate your helping. I'll bring him over directly," Gideon said and took his leave.

Doc and Henry were at the jail keeping Finnie company when Gideon arrived. Both of them were freshly groomed and smelling of tonic from a trip to the barbershop. Henry was busy showing the Indian boy his pocket watch. He would tap on the watch's crystal and then point out the window at the sun before making a sweeping motion to the west with his arm. The boy watched intently, but his face gave no indication that he had caught the drift of what Henry tried to convey.

"Pastor Roberts is going to take the boy," Gideon said as he pulled his hat off his head and dropped into his chair.

"Well, that's one less worry," Finnie said.

"I've got some good news," Doc said. "Lloyd Peabody came in this morning to get – well, never mind what he needed treating. I think you know him. He moved here a couple of years ago to take care of his older brother, Edgar. Both of them were good men. Edgar has since died, but Lloyd decided he liked Last Stand and stayed here. He's really made himself a part of the community. Lloyd is a widower. We got to talking today and he told me his wife was a Ute squaw that couldn't speak a lick of English, so he always talked to her in her language. He said he could still do it."

Gideon let out a whistle. "Good God, Doc, I could have taught that boy English in the time it took you to get around to the point of all that rambling."

"You're insufferable, Gideon Johann. I don't know why I ever try to help you. See if I do the next time you need me."

"I might as well stop by and see Lloyd on the way to take the boy to Pastor Roberts. Lloyd can explain to him what is happening and when we'll take him home. I'm not quite sure which house Lloyd lives in. Can somebody point me to the right home," Gideon said, standing and grabbing his hat.

"Come on, I'll walk you down there," Doc said.

The offer caused Gideon to grin, but he held his tongue.

Doc peered at the sheriff. "Yeah, I know I'm helping you, but if you say one word, I swear to God I'll teach Henry how to make a steer out of you."

After everybody else had left the jail, Finnie picked up a chair and carried it into the cell room. He placed it in front of Landon Noble's cell and sat down. Without saying a word, he stared at the prisoner.

Landon began to get uncomfortable from the deputy's behavior. He sat up on his cot and didn't seem to know where to look as he tried to avoid making eye contact with Finnie. Finally, the silence became too much, he blurted out, "Why are you staring at me?"

"I'm just sitting here thinking what a pleasure it will be to hang you. I'm going to make sure I'm the one that gets to slip the noose around your neck."

The comment unnerved Landon. He jumped up and started pacing back and forth across the cell. "That was a vile thing to say."

"I got back from a trip yesterday and had to watch my wife cry herself to sleep last night because she missed Charlotte so much and felt guilty that she wasn't there for her in her time of need. She is haunted by the thought of the fear Charlotte had to feel as she died."

"I'm telling you that you have the wrong man. I was sweet on Charlotte. She was nice to me. I wouldn't have hurt her for nothing."

"So you say, but the evidence says otherwise. A man that does what you did to a helpless young girl deserves to rot in Hell."

Landon rushed to the cell door and gripped a bar with each hand as he pressed his face against the iron. "I swear to you on my mother's grave that I never laid a hand on Charlotte. The only thing I did was take a rifle that I rightly won in a poker game."

"So you say," Finnie hollered again. He grabbed the chair, marched out of the room, and slammed the door shut.

By the time Gideon returned, Finnie's anger had subsided, replaced by melancholy. He thought he'd been handling Charlotte's death pretty well, but the combination of Mary's despair and the conversation with Landon had ripped the scab from the wound again. His emotions were raw and made him painfully aware of how much he missed the young girl.

"Are you all right?" Gideon asked after noticing that the usually verbose Irishman was awfully quiet.

"I'm fine. Just feeling sore from the fight today. How did things go with the boy?" Finnie asked to change the subject.

"Actually, quite good. Lloyd was able to make him understand that we would return him to the reservation after we found more of the boys. His name translates to Falling Sky. Thank goodness we know that because I sure as hell can't pronounce his real name."

"Glad to hear it."

"Are you sure you are all right?   You act like somebody shot your dog and stole your favorite dolly."

"Nah, I'm fine."

When Gideon saw that the teasing didn't so much as make Finnie stir, he knew something was wrong with his friend. He had known Finnie enough years to know when to prod and when to leave well enough alone. Today was a day to let things be. "I think I'm going to make a walk of the town and see what's going on. I'm sure the mayor and everybody else will have some gossip for me."

"Sounds about right. I'll stay here and hold down the fort," Finnie said with a nod of his head.

Gideon walked outside and headed down the street. He strolled past the entrance to the Last Chance before hesitating and letting out a sigh. After spinning around on his heels, he marched into the saloon and found Mary behind the bar and Delta waiting tables. Gideon sat down at his usual table as Mary came hustling over with a beer. With their routine established years ago, she took a seat without prompting.

"So, what brings you in, and where is my husband?" Mary asked.

"He's back at the jail," Gideon answered and took a swig of beer.

"Did you find any of the Indian boys today?"

"We found one. Finnie had to kill the miner."

"Is Finnie all right?" Mary asked, concern in her voice.

"Oh, he's fine. Maybe a little sore from the fight. He didn't listen to me and did what I planned on doing."

"You like it that Finnie thinks for himself. You wouldn't have it any other way."

"That's all true, but don't tell him. He doesn't need any encouragement."

"So, what's troubling you?"

A droll smile came upon Gideon. He really did detest the way Mary could always read his moods. If he didn't know better, he would swear she could read minds or at least his. "Finnie's mood changed all at once. His spirits sank like a rock in a pond. He didn't want to talk, and I didn't push the matter. I'm not used to seeing him that way."

"Oh . . . I had a good cry about Charlotte last night. I could see I upset Finnie, but I couldn't help myself. If I had to guess, I would say I shattered his pretending to be doing fine with her death."

"Are you two going to be all right?"

Mary reached over and patted Gideon's hand. "Of course, we are. These things just take time. Think how long you all mourned Tess's death. That was every bit as bad, if not more so, of a tragedy."

Gideon picked up the mug and chugged down the rest of his beer. "I suppose you have a point. The only thing worse than Finnie being his loud, obnoxious self is his being quiet. It's like wearing a boot that doesn't fit."

"You'll be complaining to me about his sayings about whores before you know it."

"Probably so. I'll be seeing you," Gideon said. He left the saloon and made a walk of the town, catching up on the news with the townsfolk until making his way back to the jail.

Gideon gave Finnie the afternoon off to spend time with Sam with instructions to return to make a check of the town in the evening after dark. When the clock struck five o'clock, Gideon headed for the door. He put Norse into a trot as he rode for home.

Finnie returned to the jail after supper. The time with Sam had buoyed his spirits, and when Doc came over, he gladly accepted the challenge of a round of checkers. With his mood greatly improved, Finnie needled the old doctor the entire time and received as good as he gave. He won the first two games and the doctor won the last one. After they put the game board away, Doc left with Henry in tow for his usual evening at the Last Chance.

To pass the time, Finnie opened up a fresh batch of wanted posters that had arrived in the mail that day. In them, he found a new poster for Fred Parsons. The reward had been raised to $2000 after robberies in Durango and Pagosa Springs that were suspected to be at the hands of the outlaw. The eerily accurate drawing of Fred gave Finnie pause. He had a bad feeling Gideon and he would cross paths with their old friend before all was said and done, and it would not end well. After neatly pinning the new posters to the wall and removing the out-of-date ones, Finnie headed to the Corner Saloon.

The place wasn't packed with miners, but it had a good crowd for a Tuesday evening. All eyes fell on Finnie as he walked through the door and the crowd went silent. The miners were a brazen bunch and they boldly continued their hard stares.

"I heard that you or your sheriff killed Dexter Horner today," a miner challenged.

"I did. He didn't give me any choice. It was either kill or be killed," Finnie answered in a calm tone.

"Why are you picking on us prospectors? We're just trying to make a living."

"Dexter had bought an Indian boy. I fought in a war to end such things. We weren't even going to arrest him. We just wanted the boy back."

"Why do you care? He's just an Injun."

"I don't think any of you would like to be stolen and sold. An Indian doesn't either. They're really not that much different than you or me."

"A damn Injun lover. I bet you got you a squaw, too."

"Keep running your mouth and I'll show you what I've got," Finnie threatened. "I'm telling any of you that have bought these Indian boys that you best just bring them to the jail and turn them over. We aren't going to charge you with anything, but we are going to find all the boys one way or the other."

"You're awfully cocky for a little man," the miner continued.

"Take a step my way if you want to see if I can back up my words."

The warning caused the miner to avert his eyes and look down at his feet. He didn't speak.

"That's what I thought," Finnie said and walked out into the dark cloudy night.

Finnie took a few steps down the boardwalk when he heard a commotion behind him. As he spun around to see what was happening, the sound of breaking of glass signaled the demise of the streetlamp. In the shadowy light, he saw several figures charging toward him. Finnie drew back his fist and smashed it into the nose of the first man that reached him. He could feel the cartilage give way as the nose flattened into the man's face. The assailant let out a yell and dropped as if he had been shot, but before Finnie could strike again, the others overran him. They began pummeling him with blows and kicks. He managed to land a few licks, but the beating came from every direction and overwhelmed him. His knees got wobbly and then a fist to the temple sent him crashing to the ground. He endured a few more kicks until losing consciousness.

Blood draining down Finnie's throat began to suffocate him. He woke up from a coughing fit and rolled onto his stomach to clear his air passage. With what little strength he still possessed, he crawled out into the light of the nearest working streetlamp and fired his revolver into the air.

The shots caused the crowd from the Last Chance to come running to see what had happened. Somebody spotted Finnie lying in the street and hollered for Doc and Mary to come.

Mary reached Finnie before the doctor did. She let out a gasp at the sight of her bloodied husband and got down on the ground to cradle his head. "What have they done to you?" she asked between sobs.

"It looks worse than it is," Finnie whispered.

Doc slowly shuffled up to the couple. "Christ Almighty," he swore. He pulled his keys from his pocket and handed them to Henry. "Go get the stretcher. I don't want to take a chance on a broken rib puncturing his lungs."

Mary reached over and grabbed Doc's hand. "You have to fix him," she implored.

"Don't you worry about that. You know I will. Finnie is a tough one and we'll get him through this."

Finnie raised a shaky hand into the air and pointed at the doctor. "I would have been nicer during checkers if

I knew I'd be needing you," he said and forced a smile onto his bloody face.

Chapter 14

Gideon made it to town half an hour later than usual. Ever since he and Finnie had returned from the reservation, he had ignored Abby's requests to have kindling carried from the woodpile into the kitchen. Her warning at the breakfast table that there would be no more hot meals until she had some wood to cook with had prompted an end to his tardiness in the chore and made him late to work. As Gideon neared the jail, he found it odd that no smoke was coming from the stove he and Finnie used to make coffee each morning. All the years of using his intuitions to survive had given Gideon a keen sense as to when something didn't feel right. A chill ran down his back as he scanned up and down the street, noticing the broken streetlamp. He tied Norse in front of the doctor's office and rushed inside the building. Doc and Mary were sitting in chairs next to Finnie's bed. They nervously turned their heads to see who had arrived.

"What happened?" Gideon asked, alarm in his voice.

"Oh, Gideon, miners beat Finnie last night. Look what they did to him," Mary said as she rushed into Gideon's arms.

As Gideon hugged Mary and patted her back, he glanced over her shoulder at Finnie. The little Irishman turned his head to look their direction, but his eyes were so swollen that Gideon wasn't even sure Finnie could see them. The doctor had taped Finnie's broken nose in place. Between the tape, bruising, and swelling, Finnie was unrecognizable. Gideon took a slow deep breath in hopes of calming his churning stomach. He concentrated on comforting Mary to keep from throwing up.

"How bad is it?" Gideon asked Doc.

"He has a concussion and blood in his urine. They worked him over good. He won't be doing any Irish jigs for a week or two."

"I'm not dead. I can speak for myself," Finnie complained in a raised voice that sounded mumbled by puffy lips. He grimaced in pain when he finished speaking.

Mary released her grip on Gideon, allowing him to go to his friend's side.

"Did you get a good look at who did this?" Gideon asked.

Finnie reached up and rubbed his throbbing temple before speaking. "It was too dark after they broke the streetlamp. There must have been four or five of them. One of them is sporting a flat nose today. I got him good. I got in a few more good licks, but there were just too many of them. I went into the Corner Saloon beforehand. They were all riled over Dexter getting himself killed."

Gideon lightly patted Finnie's shoulder. His friend looked as if he might disintegrate if touched too forcefully. Out of habit, Gideon rubbed the scar on his cheek as he tried to control the rage building inside him. "I'm sorry for leaving you alone last night. I never dreamed those prospectors would do something like this. Those boys are barking up the wrong tree if they think they can get by with beating you."

"It's not your fault. I would have never guessed it either or else I would have been more careful. I should have known yesterday wasn't my day when Dexter nearly got the best of me."

"You just rest. I'll check in with you later."

After Gideon told the others goodbye, he marched toward the door as if on a mission. Mary came scurrying after him and grabbed his sleeve, pulling him to a stop.

"Gideon, don't you dare go doing something stupid by yourself. We don't need both of you busted up. Finnie is more than enough," Mary warned.

"Don't you worry about that. Those boys will be dealing with me on my terms and won't get the chance to gang up on me like they did Finnie – I promise. I feel terrible for not seeing this coming. Just take care of him."

"I will. Don't forget what I told you."

Gideon nodded his head and disappeared out the door. He mounted Norse and raced to the general store. After jogging inside, he strode to the aisle where the store had a barrel of ax handles. He picked through them until he found one that he liked its weight and balance when he shook it in his hand.

On his way past the counter, Gideon held up the handle for the store owner, Mayor Hiram Howard, to see. "Put this on the county's tab. This is for official business," he said, leaving the mayor with a puzzled expression. Before Hiram could ask a question, Gideon was gone.

Gideon pointed Norse toward the river and gave the horse free rein. The animal gaited into a nice lope that was easy to fall into rhythm with. Norse had definitely inherited his daddy's gift for endurance as well as speed. Sometimes it felt to Gideon as if the horse could go all day at this pace. When they reached the river, Gideon turned the horse onto the trail along the water. He planned to find the man with the smashed nose to get the names of the others from him. As Gideon passed miners panning the river, most would stop and watch him go by. One prospector made a point of looking away, causing Gideon to suspect him of being one of those responsible for Finnie's beating. Gideon also saw an Indian boy standing in the river while panning for gold. Rescuing the boy would have to wait.

While Gideon sped along the river, he spotted a man standing in the river a good eighth of a mile away. The man saw Gideon too and took off running for a horse tied at the river's edge. He jumped on the animal and headed straight south toward the foothills. Gideon tapped the rein against Norse's neck to turn the horse in a southwest direction in hopes of catching the fleeing miner. Norse cut so quickly that Gideon nearly lost his balance in the saddle. The horse had not only inherited his stallion's speed and endurance, but also his mustang mare's natural agility culled from generations of surviving in the wild. Gideon had never galloped Norse on anything but roadway and had no inkling on how the horse would react to the rough terrain. At that moment, he didn't care. Avenging Finnie's beating was all that mattered.

Norse flawlessly navigated the treacherous ground, dodging rocks and crevices as he zigged and zagged onward. Up ahead, Gideon spotted a gulch that had to be at least five feet wide and deep enough that he couldn't see the bottom. He had no idea if Norse would jump the gully, but he didn't try to slow the horse. If Norse came to an abrupt stop, Gideon figured he'd go sailing over the horse's head and probably break his neck. As they rapidly advanced upon the gulch, Gideon took a deep breath and prepared for whatever came next. Norse never even broke stride as he launched into the air. His feet touched the ground without so much as a jolt to his rider.

The miner's horse was starting to slow. With the pace Norse was setting, Gideon judged he would catch his quarry perfectly from the side. He gave the horse free rein and waited. When they had closed to within twenty yards of the other horse, the prospector drew his revolver and fired. The shot missed. Norse didn't flinch but pinned his ears back and burst into an even faster pace. With the horse having passed every other test, Gideon decided to try one last thing. Before a second shot was fired, he steered Norse, so the horse's flank bumped the other horse. The force of the collision sent the other animal tumbling and caused the miner to sail from the saddle. He landed hard on the ground and rolled. With ax handle in hand, Gideon jumped from Norse and charged the prone man. The miner flopped onto his back and raised his gun. A swing of the club sent the revolver flying through the air, causing the prospector to swear a blue streak from the pain of his smashed fingers.

"How do you like a little beating?" Gideon screamed as he waylaid the miner again and again with the handle. He avoided the man's head, preferring the meaty parts of the arms and legs to avoid breaking any bones.

"Stop. Stop, you're going to kill me," the miner cried out.

Gideon swung the ax handle one more time, landing against the miner's knee and causing more swearing. He stood over the cowering prospector and tried to catch his breath. From the looks of the man's nose, he knew he had the guilty party.

"I'm going to ask you one time for the names of the other men that beat my deputy. If you don't tell me, I swear to God I'll finish you off with this club," Gideon warned between gasps of air. He shook the club at the miner.

"I'll tell you. I'll tell you. Just don't hit me again. It was Jimbo Wright, Clancy Storm, and Willard Huff."

Gideon raised his club over his head. "Was there anybody else?"

The miner covered his head with his arms. "No. I swear to God there wasn't."

"If you're still in my county by tomorrow, I'm coming back to kill you with this axe handle. Do I make myself clear?"

"I don't even know if I can get on my horse after the beating you've given me."

"Good. I'd rather kill you anyway," Gideon said and retrieved the miner's revolver. He unloaded the gun and tossed it. He then did the same with the prospector's rifle. "You're lucky your horse looks to be fine. You best be gone."

The miner hobbled to his feet. "I will be."

Gideon walked over to Norse and rubbed the horse's nose. "I'll never be able to tell you you're a better horse than old Buck was – me and him spent too many nights together when I didn't have a friend in the world except for him, but I'm telling you right now that you are one fine horse. I need to write Caleb and tell him what a great horse he sent my way. Let's ride, boy – nice and easy this time."

Before dusk had completely settled over the land, Gideon had managed to track down all three of the other attackers of Finnie. While they all acted skittish around the sheriff, none were wise enough to suspect they had been sold out or to lie about their name. Their response was answered with the ax handle. Gideon gave each of the miners a beating and a warning to be gone by sunup.

By the time Gideon made it back to town, nightfall had arrived. He found Henry sitting with Finnie in the doctor's office. Doc was out on a call and Mary had returned to work at the Last Chance. Finnie was sitting up in bed, looking more alive than he had in the morning.

"How are you feeling?" Gideon asked.

"Better than a day spent riding with you," Finnie joked.

Gideon grinned and held up the ax handle. "I have a souvenir for you. This here handle gave a whipping to four men today. They best be gone by morning."

Finnie tilted his head to see better through the slits of his swollen eyes. "You got all of them?"

"I believe so."

"Thank you, Gideon. I surely appreciate you doing that."

"You'd have done the same for me – just used your fist instead of cheating like I did. By the way, I know where another boy is. I just couldn't get to him today with this going on."

"We'll get them when I'm better. As soon as the swelling goes out of my eyes and I quit pissing blood, I'll be ready to go."

"Just take it easy. We don't need you to have a setback."

"Hey, Gideon, I've been meaning to tell you we got a new poster on Fred. He's robbing around Durango and Pagosa Springs."

Gideon shook his head and took a seat. He had been fearing such news would reach him. "Maybe he'll stay away. I really don't want to deal with him."

"Who is Fred?" Henry asked.

With a sigh, Gideon said, "Fred Parsons used to ride with Finnie and me in the war. He saved my life once. Now he's an outlaw. It's a sad deal."

"So, you feel a loyalty to him even though he's an outlaw?"

Gideon nodded his head.

"Will you arrest him if he comes to Last Stand?"

Gideon looked at Finnie and then toward Henry. "I just hope he doesn't show up here."

Chapter 15

With all the summer rain, the grazing land stayed green and growing, and the creeks and streams were running plenty of good water. The ideal weather provided Ethan more free time than usual for the month of July. He didn't have to worry about moving his herds to fresh grass or away from stagnant water.

After Sarah and Sylvia headed to town for supplies on the buckboard, Ethan decided to take Benjamin fishing at their pond. He strapped a bucket of worms to his saddle horn, and with fishing poles in hand, they set out for the watering hole with Benjamin's dog, Chase, following them.

The father and son reached the pond and took seats on the bank so that the sun shined on their faces. With the warm summer air and the cloudless, robin-egg-blue sky, the day seemed perfect for fishing. In a half an hour, they had three good-sized bluegills to show for their efforts. Neither of them had hardly uttered a word as they concentrated on their lines.

Benjamin finally looked up and studied the massive mountains in the background a moment before he broke the silence. "By the time you were my age did you know you wanted to be a rancher?"

Ethan pulled his pipe from his pocket, packed it with tobacco, and lit it. "Yeah, I guess I did. Gideon and I had all these plans of ranching together. We planned on having the biggest spread in the Colorado Territory." He chuckled at the memory.

"That probably would have happened if Gideon hadn't accidentally killed that little boy during the war and stayed away from here for all those years."

Ethan took a puff on his pipe and tilted his head up as he blew out a plume of smoke. "I don't know about us being the biggest ranch around, but I suspect we would have gone into ranching together."

Benjamin caught another bluegill and the conversation was interrupted while he took it off the hook, rebaited, and threw his line back out into the water. "Does it make you sad to think about what might have been?" he asked.

Glancing over at his son, Ethan was reminded again that Benjamin was a very thoughtful person for one so young. "It really bothered me when Gideon first came back and got his life straightened out. I kept stewing over all the years of his life that were wasted while he ran from his past while we could have been ranching together and being friends, but then I realized I should just be grateful that Gideon found himself and he's back in our lives. All in all, things have worked out just fine."

"Gideon isn't like most people, is he?" Benjamin asked as he scratched Chase behind the ear. "He's loyal like a dog."

Ethan let out a laugh. "I doubt he'd appreciate you comparing him to a dog, but you do have a point. Gideon would get up off his deathbed if we needed him."

"Pa, would you be really sad if I didn't go into ranching with you? I have all these stories in my head that need to come out. I want to be a writer like Mark Twain."

The change of direction of the conversation took Ethan by surprise. He looked over at Benjamin and felt a little crushed his son didn't possess the same love for ranching that he did. His disappointment was quickly overwhelmed with pride that Benjamin was his own man with his own passions. "I'll be proud of you no matter what career you choose as long as you put your heart into it and be the best you can be. You need to start writing now and get those stories down on paper and out of your head. That's how you'll learn and get better."

"You mean it?"

Ethan nodded his head. "You still have to help me around here though. An author needs plenty of real-life experiences before he can write a masterpiece," he said and winked.

"I feel so much better. I've been wanting to talk to you about this for a while, but I've dreaded it so. I know it's not what you want, but I'm just sure I'm supposed to be a writer."

A fish on Ethan's line brought a halt to the conversation. By the time the bluegill was added to the string of fish and Ethan had returned his line into the water, the moment between father and son seemed to have passed and they fell silent again.

After a few minutes had lapsed, Benjamin blurted out, "Do you think Winnie and I will marry someday?"

The question caused Ethan to pull his head back and then look at his son with an amused expression. "How would I know? I would think you and Winnie would have a much better idea to the answer to that question than me."

"I just wondered what other people thought," Benjamin said, shrugging his shoulders.

"Well, I will tell you that is a hot subject amongst people, especially our church members. There's a chance you and Winnie will decide that you two were meant for each other or there may come a day when one of you decides you want to know what it feels like to meet somebody new. Either way, I feel certain you'll be friends forever."

"I suppose you're right, but I can't imagine ever wanting any girl besides Winnie. I kissed her the other day," Benjamin said matter-of-factly.

"I thought you did that when you were eight."

"I mean I really kissed her."

Ethan could feel his face turning red. The confession embarrassed him something terrible and made him uncomfortable, though a surge of satisfaction gushed through him that his son could talk so openly with his father. "Oh," he said and paused. "If we catch a few more fish, we'll have enough for dinner tonight."

∞

Sarah had finished her shopping at the dry goods and general stores. She bought Sylvia a peppermint stick as she paid for her last purchases as a reward for helping clean the house that morning. After putting the bundles into the wagon, they headed to the greengrocery. As Sarah picked through the produce, she looked around and discovered Sylvia was gone. The disappearance didn't concern her until she realized the child was nowhere to be found inside the store. She ran outside and looked up and down the street, and still didn't see her daughter. With her heart starting to race, Sarah ran to the dry goods store, and after being assured the child was not there, she dashed into the general store. The clerk was getting ready to exchange a sack of licorice for the penny Sylvia held up for him. Sarah grabbed Sylvia by the hand and yanked her out of the store before the purchase transpired.

"Young lady, where did you get that money?" Sarah barked once they were by the wagon.

"I found it on the floor of the green store," Sylvia answered.

Sarah grabbed Sylvia under the arms and hoisted her onto the wagon seat. "If you know what's good for you, you'll keep your butt in this seat until I get back," she warned.

The incident had scared Sarah so badly that she felt weak all over. Her anger made her fearful she'd say something she would regret. Having already lived through the kidnapping of Benjamin years ago, the incident brought back a flood of bad memories. She turned and marched back to the greengrocery and quickly made her purchase.

On the trip home, mother and daughter sat silently. Sarah had calmed herself for the most part but decided to let Sylvia stew a while longer before she lit into her.

Sylvia couldn't stand the silence any longer. She knew she was in big trouble, but she just wanted to get whatever was coming her way over with and to be done with the whole thing. "I was buying the licorice for Benjamin. I don't even like it. If you thought I stole that penny – well, that's something I wouldn't ever do. You and Pa have taught me better than that."

Sarah looked over at her daughter and then turned her attention back to steering the horses. She still wasn't ready to say her piece about the matter.

A single sob escaped Sylvia. She had been trying to hold it in but couldn't contain it any longer. All the silence from her momma began to make her panic. She looked over at Sarah and asked, "Are you going to send me away?"

The question so overwhelmed Sarah that her eyes immediately welled with tears. She pulled the horses to a stop and set the brake before turning toward her daughter and grasping her by the shoulders. "You scared me so badly today. I feared somebody might have stolen you. I'm still so mad at you that I could pinch your little head off, but, Sylvia, I love you just as much as I do Benjamin. We would never ever, ever send you away. There will probably come a day when you wish we would, but you are stuck with us forever – that is a promise. Do you understand me?"

Sylvia nodded her head and burst into tears. Stifling her own urge to cry, Sarah pulled her daughter into her bosom and patted her back.

"You have to promise me you won't ever wander off from me again. Then we're going to forget this whole thing ever happened and have smiles on our faces when we get home."

"I promise."

∞

Sarah fried the fish that night, and the family had enjoyed the change in diet. Ethan and Benjamin had both been effusive in their praise of the meal.

Afterward, the family spent most of the evening playing lively games of dominoes. Once the children had gone to bed, Sarah nestled against Ethan on the sofa, resting her head upon his shoulder.

"Did you and Benjamin have a good day together?" Sarah asked.

Ethan let out a little chuckle. "Yes, we did, but it came at a cost. Benjamin told me what he wants to be when he grows up. He wants to be a writer."

The news didn't really shock Sarah. She had sensed that the day was coming when Benjamin would have a talk with his father. The only part that surprised her a little was Benjamin wanting to be an author. She had suspected he might think of becoming a lawyer. "How do you feel about that?" she asked.

"Oh, I'm disappointed, but I'm at peace with the idea. I want him to find his place in the world and not settle for what I want him to be."

"Good. I'm glad he feels like he can talk to you. That shows you how much he loves and respects you."

Ethan thought about telling his wife about the conversation he and Benjamin had had concerning Winnie but decided to keep the topic a private one between father and son. "How was your day with Sylvia?"

The question brought a smile to Sarah's face. The incident that day didn't seem near as monumental as it had at the moment it had happened. After her anxiety had faded, she had even been impressed that the child planned to use the penny for Benjamin's sake. She had already decided not to tell Ethan about what Sylvia had done that day. Some things were best left just between a mother and her daughter. "Oh, I think we had a pretty good one. Sylvia really is a thoughtful child."

Chapter 16

While Finnie dealt with some dizzy spells and soreness as he continued to recover at home, Gideon spent extra time in town to cover for the loss of his deputy. The sheriff suffered from a bad case of a guilty conscience. Gideon knew Finnie didn't blame him for what had happened, but he blamed himself. Abby had preached to him that Finnie's beating wasn't his fault until she was exasperated, but he needed to hear it from Mary. He slipped into the back room of the Last Chance to find her paying her whiskey supplier. The notion to wait outside until they were finished conducting business never occurred to him and he took a seat to wait until the man left the saloon.

When the supplier had finally gone, Mary took a seat across the table from Gideon. She couldn't help but smile at his display of familiarity. For someone so smart, he could still be just another clueless man. "And to what do I owe this pleasure?" she asked.

Gideon adjusted his butt in the chair before speaking. "I thought I would check in and see how Finnie felt this morning."

"You know you can walk to our house and ask him in person. I talked Doc into letting him go back to the jail tomorrow as long as he takes it easy. About one more day in the house and he is going to drive me and Mrs. Penny crazy."

"Great. Now he can wear me out with some pointless story."

"All right, we've known each other way too long for small talk. Why are you really here?"

Gideon rolled his eyes and shook his head. Sometimes he liked to pretend he was clueless as to why he subjected himself to Mary's inquisitions even though he knew darn well why he put himself through it. "Because I feel guilty for what happened to Finnie. And you're the lucky one I always choose to talk about these things, especially since he is your husband."

The confession prompted Mary to shake her head and give a wry smile. "I don't know why I even had to ask. I should have known. Gideon, I hate to break it to you, but you are not some Greek god that can always come to everyone's rescue – you just think you are. You had no way of knowing those miners would do something so foolish. The main thing is Finnie will be fine in a few days. Quit beating yourself up. It doesn't become you. Finnie doesn't blame you and I certainly don't either."

Gideon sighed. "Thank you. I think I just needed to hear from you that you didn't blame me. I do think I make a pretty good Greek god though."

Mary let out a giggle. "Of course, you do. After all, you are the legendary Gideon Johann."

Gideon mockingly nodded his head before turning serious. "I wish the judge would hurry up and get here. I'd like to get Landon Noble convicted of killing Charlotte."

"Do you feel certain he did it?"

"I think so. All the evidence points that way even if it isn't clear-cut."

"Finnie is sure ready to hang him. I've never seen him be so bitter. This one is certainly personal."

"That it is. Maybe we can all get on with our lives after we get Charlotte some justice."

"I suppose, but nothing is going to bring that girl back." Mary paused as she reflected on her dead friend. "I think about her every day."

"How is Juanita working out on running the café?"

"She's doing a fine job. The new waitress is another matter. I hear grumblings in the saloon all the time about her messing up orders. I like her though and tell everyone to be patient. I think she'll get there."

"I guess I had better go earn my keep. Thanks for the chat even if I think you're getting meaner in your old age," Gideon said as he stood.

"If you ever use my name and the term 'old age' in another sentence, you'll be resting in the cemetery. I'm just as close to your oldest daughter's age as I am yours."

"Ouch. I didn't need to be reminded of that. See, you are getting mean. I'll catch you later."

Gideon returned to the jail to find the attorney, Billy Todd, waiting there. The lawyer was an affable enough fellow that had never given the sheriff any problems while representing prisoners locked there. In fact, Gideon would go as far as to say he liked Billy despite his profession.

"Hey, Billy. I guess you're here to talk to Landon again," Gideon said, retrieving the keys to the cells before the lawyer could answer.

"That I am," Billy replied and followed Gideon back to the cell room where the sheriff locked him in with Landon Noble.

Gideon returned to his desk and began doing paperwork. He had lost track of time when Billy finally hollered for him. After glancing at the clock, he retrieved the lawyer. Billy followed Gideon back into the room, and to the surprise of the sheriff, took a seat.

The lawyer set his satchel across his lap and flopped his arms down on it. "You know, Gideon, I've never said this before to you and I doubt I'll ever say it again, but I don't think Landon killed Charlotte. There is nothing about his personality to suggest he is a killer – especially a cold-blooded one. He is too soft. And besides, he swears up and down he didn't do it even after I told him that a lawyer needs to know the truth to better defend his client."

"I agree with you that he doesn't come off as a murderer. I think it was a clumsy crime of passion after getting rejected by Charlotte. He certainly is adamant about his innocence, I'll give him that." Gideon leaned back in his chair and rubbed his neck.

"I guess we'll see what a jury believes. I just told you this because I think you should keep your eyes open for another suspect. I hope I haven't offended you."

"No, not at all. I want to hang Charlotte's killer, but I sure want it to be the right man. I'll keep what you said in mind, but until something suggests otherwise, I still think Landon did it."

"You have a good day. I'll be seeing you soon," Billy said and took his leave.

No sooner had Billy departed than Gideon heard the door opening again. He looked up, expecting to see the lawyer returning but instead found Doc and Henry entering the jail.

"We just got back from checking on Finnie. He's doing much better," Doc said while taking a seat.

"I hear I get the pleasure of babysitting him starting tomorrow," Gideon said.

"I think so. He doesn't need to be chasing any bank robbers, but he can sit in here just as well as he can his own house."

"That's special. Just be sure to come over and distract him for part of the day since you caved in to Mary." Gideon gave the doctor a smug look.

"I'd rather have you mad at me than her. She's the one that pours my beers. Finnie needs to get to doing something anyway. You know you can't really hurt an Irishman by hitting him in the head."

"I can't believe you said that," Gideon said with astonishment in his voice that the doctor would actually say such a thing.

"Oh, I was only joking. Quit being so darn serious. I can always tell when you have a guilty conscience because you lose all sense of humor. He is going to be fine so stop blaming yourself."

"I suppose you have a point, but things like that sound better when I say them instead of a Harvard man."

"Henry is the Harvard man. These days I'm just the old man," Doc mused.

The door to the jail flew open and Oscar Fry rushed in. The small-time rancher looked to be in a panic. "Thelma is in labor and the baby is breech. She sent me for you,"

Doc rubbed his face for a moment before glancing over at his grandson. "Henry, I would love to take you with me and show you how to turn a baby, but Thelma is only letting me see her because she is desperate.

There is no way in hell she would let you into the room. You might as well stay in town."

Henry nodded his head.

Gideon stood and headed for the door. "I'll go to the livery and get your rig ready while you get whatever you need at your office. I'm staying in town this evening. Henry can dine with me at the café."

"Thank you, Gideon," Doc said as he tried to get around Oscar as the man nervously hopped about and twitched.

After Doc and Oscar had left town, Gideon and Henry headed to Mary's café. The new waitress came to their table. Carla was a pretty and vivacious girl with auburn hair and green eyes. While she took their orders, she kept smiling at Henry.

"I think you could get you a girlfriend if you wanted," Gideon teased.

"I don't think courting was included in my reasons for getting to spend my summer here. Mother would probably kill me," Henry said with a grin.

"Well, mothers don't have to know everything." Gideon gave Henry a wink.

"How did you and Grandpa become such good friends?"

Gideon leaned the chair back on two legs and rubbed his scar as he thought about the question. "Well, I've known him all my life and he's saved my butt on a couple of occasions. That certainly didn't hurt. I guess mainly it is the fact I'm drawn to people that speak their mind. And Doc has on more than one occasion told me how it is. I respect that about him. I suppose the other thing is we just enjoy each other's company. We're certainly not as odd of a pair as Doc and Finnie. Now those two are as different as Boston and Last Stand.

Henry grinned at the analogy. "Speaking of those towns, I'm thinking of moving here and going into practice with Grandpa when I'm done with school."

"Really? You'd leave your family back east for Last Stand?"

"I just love it here and being with Grandpa. The cool evenings, the air as sweet as candy, and getting up in the mornings and seeing the mountains off in the distance. What's not to love?"

Gideon solemnly nodded his head as he contemplated what he was about to say. "I hope I'm not overstepping my bounds, but I have something I want to say. I would personally love for you to come here, but you know, your grandpa is getting old. I hate to say this, but realistically, you could get out here and end up being alone after a while. Doc may outlive me, and then again, he might not."

"I've thought about that, but I'd like to spend as much time with him as possible. He and my family were both robbed of time together. I could always move back home if I got lonely or Mother and Father could move here after Father retires. I think he'll quit the banking business as soon as he feels my sister is old enough to run things."

"Just so you've reasoned everything out. I guess I need to give you some more shooting lessons. Out here, every man needs to know how to use a gun."

"I would like that. Finnie is going to teach me to box."

"He's the best. Does your mother know that?"

Henry shook his head as Carla returned with the meals. She gave Henry the steak Gideon had ordered and placed Henry's meatloaf in front of the sheriff. They waited until she left to switch plates.

As Gideon began cutting his steak, he said, "You know that women can be slim pickings around here. That's an itch that eventually has to be scratched."

Henry let out a giggle and colored a little at the comment. "So I've noticed. I guess there is always Carla if I don't get too fussy about getting the food I ordered. She certainly is pretty. Mother worked as a waitress. That's how she stole Father's heart."

The two continued their conversation, talking mostly about Gideon's various treks into the mountains. When they finished their food, Gideon paid for the meals. Henry left to return to Doc's office while Gideon made a walk of the town as the sun sunk below the horizon.

While Gideon strolled Last Stand, some of the prospectors were making their way toward the Corner Saloon. Word of the beatings the sheriff had handed out had spread amongst the men. Gideon could feel the hostility as the miners passed by him, refusing to look his way.

Gideon returned to the jail and finished the paperwork he never got the chance to complete earlier. Afterward, he walked to the Last Chance. With Finnie at home, Doc delivering a baby, and Mary too busy to sit with him, Gideon passed the time talking to some of the regulars. Making small talk with acquaintances had never been his strong suit. Truth be told, he would have just as soon sat by himself but felt obligated to make conversation since he served as sheriff. Gideon was in the process of trying to extract himself from a ranch hand talking incessantly about cattle when the crack of a gunshot carried into the saloon.

As Gideon dashed into the street, he heard the clomping of a horse galloping away into the night. Patrons were streaming out of the Corner Saloon and calling for help. Deciding to forgo chasing the escapee, Gideon jogged into the saloon instead. A man lay sprawled on the floor with a gunshot to the arm. The bartender held a blood-soaked towel against the wound while other miners stood around watching

Gideon wondered sometimes if the prospectors were smart enough to get out of the rain. "Well, some of you pick him up and carry the man to the doctor's office. You can't just stand there and watch him bleed to death," he barked.

The command set the miners into motion and they hoisted the man off the floor.

"So, what happened?" Gideon asked as he walked with the men toward the doctor's office.

"Noel accused Stanley of cheating at cards and Stanley up and shot him," a miner replied.

When the men entered the office, Henry jumped up from his chair, his book falling to the floor. He looked taken aback and even retreated a step before spotting Gideon coming in behind the others.

"Henry, we have a man that's shot. You are going to have to take a look at him," Gideon called out.

A look of panic came over Henry as he glanced down at the injured man. "Gideon, I'm not that far along in my training," he stammered.

"You are all we have at the moment. Just do your best. He looks as if he'll bleed to death otherwise," Gideon assured the young man.

Noel was plopped onto the examining table. The trauma had caused him to lose consciousness. With each beat of his heart, a stream of blood would shoot from the wound. As Gideon ran the other men out of the office, Henry applied a tourniquet above the wound, slowing the bleeding some. After Henry scrubbed his hands and doused them with carbolic acid, he inserted his finger into the wound, causing Noel to let out a groan.

"His humerus is shattered. I think his arm will need amputating, but there is no way I could do that. The axillary artery must be severed for there to be this much blood. Gideon, I don't know. Sewing up Carter's knife wound is the only suturing I've ever done in my life. I have no idea if I can ligate an artery. What if I fail?"

"Henry, doing nothing would be failure. Trying your best when you don't know what you are doing is not failure. It is a valiant effort."

Henry nodded his head and sprang into action. He retrieved a cloth and a bottle of chloroform. "Hold him down," he ordered while dousing the rag with the liquid.

The young man covered Noel's mouth and nose with the cloth. While Noel struggled for air, Gideon kept him pinned to the table until he grew still. Gideon, sensing that he would be needed, then scrubbed his hands and imitated Henry in covering them with the carbolic acid. After Henry took a deep breath to steady his nerves, he grabbed a scalpel and peered at the instrument a moment before glancing at Gideon.

"Gideon, please grab that towel and try to absorb the blood while I work," Henry requested.

Henry made an incision on either side of the wound to give himself room to work. After Gideon soaked up the blood, Henry found the severed artery and managed to extract its end from the surrounding tissue and to clamp it off. His hands were shaking so badly that he struggled to thread a needle with the catgut suture. He had to take a moment to calm himself. Once he had the needle prepared, he ligated the artery the way he imagined his grandfather would perform the procedure.

"I don't know if I did a single thing correctly, but I got the bleeding stopped. Thank God I got an A in anatomy," Henry said, excitement in his voice.

"You have given this man a chance. That's all that can be expected."

Henry doused the wound with carbolic acid and then bandaged it. After scrubbing the blood from his hands, he dropped into a chair. His body sagged, and he took a deep breath.

Gideon walked over and patted Henry on top of the shoulder. "I'm going to buy you a beer the first chance we get."

Henry smiled for the first time since the ordeal had begun. "Believe me, I'm going to let you."

Chapter 17

Doc didn't return to town until morning. He skipped returning his buggy to the livery stable and instead pulled the rig up to the front door of his office for fear he didn't have the stamina to make the walk. When the doctor shuffled inside, he was shocked to see Gideon and Henry sleeping in chairs and a patient in the bed. He tried to close the door quietly, but Gideon, a light sleeper from his years of living by his wits, woke as the latch clicked into place. The sheriff looked around, stretched, then tiptoed over to the doctor.

"What happened here?" Doc asked, the surprising circumstance having aroused him somewhat from his lethargy.

"A miner got shot last night. His name is Noel. Henry saved his life. He tied off some artery to get the bleeding to stop but thinks the arm will have to be amputated. During the night, he had to give Noel some laudanum to quiet him down."

The doctor's stature seemed to grow as he swelled with pride at the news. "I tell you, that boy is a natural. Thank you for staying with him."

Gideon waved his hand through the air to suggest his contribution had been of no consequence. "You should have seen Henry. He figured things out as he went and got the job done."

Doc smiled and nodded his head.

How are Thelma and the baby?"

"I think they will be fine, but it was a bad delivery and a very long night. I'm going to check this patient, and if he's stable, I'm going to bed. I'm liable to amputate the wrong arm with how I feel right now. I'm getting too old for staying up all night delivering babies that aren't ready to make their appearance into the world. Thank you, again."

"I'm going to ride home so Abby doesn't worry all day what happened to me. I planned on going home last night, but those darn miners changed all that. Afterward, I guess I need to track down the man that shot Noel. I got some decent sleep last night, but I think Henry stayed awake most of the night worrying about his patient," Gideon said while trying to stretch the kinks out of his back after spending the night in a chair.

Gideon rode home to find Abby washing up the breakfast dishes. The look of relief on her face made Gideon feel both tingly with love and guilty that his job put such stress on his wife. Abby quickly dried her hands on a towel, then wrapped her arms around Gideon.

"I hate it when you don't come home like planned," Abby said, her mouth next to Gideon's ear.

"I know you do and so do I," Gideon replied before explaining all that had happened the previous night.

"I guess that means you have to leave to find the shooter and might not be back tonight either."

"It does." Gideon nuzzled his face into her neck and kissed her. "I'm sorry."

"I'm fine as long as you're safe. Let me cook you a good breakfast. I have a bad feeling you won't be getting any warm meals for a while."

While Abby fried ham and eggs, Gideon spent time with Winnie and Chance. Winnie, with her gusto for life, was all excited about her new fascination with training their dog, Red. The dog had mastered sit, stay, and down, and Winnie insisted on demonstrating each trick to her stepfather. Chance showed off his new toy gun that Benjamin had whittled for him and brought over yesterday on his visit. The gun made Gideon smile as he rubbed his fingers down the smoothly carved barrel. He had been the one that taught Benjamin how to make something out of his whittling back when he first got to know the boy.

Abby sent the children out to play as she brought the food to the table. She took a seat across from Gideon and sipped her coffee.

Gideon savored a bite of egg, even closing his eyes as he chewed. After swallowing, he looked at Abby. "Do you ever think about all the years we lost when I was out there running from my past? So many wasted years. We might have had a whole passel of kids. Think of all the memories we never got to make."

As Abby reached over and took Gideon's hand, she gazed into his blue eyes. Even after a lifetime of knowing him, she still marveled at their deep color. His comments caused a melancholy smile. "I guess I do sometimes on bad days or those times when I don't understand you, but on most mornings, I wake up feeling blessed that we ever got a second chance. That still seems like a miracle to me. And there would be no Winnie if I had never been married to Marcus. I can't imagine life without my little bullhead. All in all, I think life turned out just fine."

Gideon gave a smile to keep his emotions under control. "I don't know what I did to deserve you – I really don't."

"I'd say we're both pretty lucky. You better eat your eggs before they get cold."

With a wink, Gideon resumed eating. When he finished, he packed some hardtack, jerky, and a change of clothes into his saddlebags. After telling the children goodbye, Gideon pulled Abby against him and hugged her.

"I'll be back as soon as I can. We need a day alone. I think the kids need to spend some time with their new niece," Gideon said with a wink. "I love you."

"I love you, too. Just be careful." Abby kissed Gideon goodbye.

Gideon rode out, headed toward the river. He hoped to learn something about the shooter from some other miner even if the odds of one of them helping seemed unlikely. The first prospector Gideon came upon was a little wiry man looking to be pushing sixty years. His back was beginning to stoop from years bent over panning for gold. Gideon remembered seeing him at the Corner Saloon the previous night. When he approached the little man, he could see the fear in his eyes – always a good sign for extracting information.

While extending his hand, Gideon greeted the miner with a conciliatory tone. "I saw you at the saloon last night. I was hoping you could tell me anything you knew about this Stanley that shot Noel."

"Is Noel going to be all right?" the miner asked in a voice surprisingly deep for his size.

"He'll more than likely lose his arm."

"That damn Stanley is an impetuous bastard – and he was cheating. His name is Stanley York. I believe he spent a lot of time up at Crested Butte. Most of the other miners aren't too fond of him. That's about all I know."

"What does he look like?"

"Like a prospector. He's about your height with a long brown beard. I'd say he's about forty if I had to guess. He rides an ancient bay mare."

"Thank you. You've been more than helpful." Gideon turned to mount Norse.

"Hey, Sheriff, I don't know if it's true, but Stanley liked to brag about his marksmanship. You might want to be careful."

"I'll keep that in mind, but if he aimed to kill Noel, he shot rather poorly last night. But on the other hand, I've known men that couldn't hit a barn with a pistol but could shave your chin with a rifle. Thanks for the tip."

As Gideon rode away, he pondered the situation. In his experience, when most people got into trouble, they tended to head to somewhere they knew. If his hunch was correct, Stanley would be going to Crested Butte. The trail between there and Last Stand was mountainous and hard traveling. There was no way Stanley could push an old mare hard through there. Unfortunately, there would also be plenty of places for an ambush. He pointed Norse to the northeast to hit the trail that headed for Crested Butte.

Knowing that the first several miles were easy traveling through ranch grazing land, Gideon put Norse into an easy lope to make some time. When he came upon the roadway going north, he spotted some tracks made by a running horse. He stopped and dismounted Norse to get a better look. The hoofprint patterns were uneven as if the horse had to adjust its gait continuously to keep up the pace. Climbing back on his horse, he resumed his pursuit. With a little luck, he figured he would encounter Stanley sooner rather than later.

The day was pleasant with just enough breeze to keep the body from getting warm while riding. Cattle herds grazed on either side of the road in tall luscious grass on the prime ranch land. Gideon's view to the north featured some of the most massive mountains surrounding Last Stand. Snow still covered their peaks, even in July. These mountains had always been his favorites. There were a lot worse things a man could be doing than riding a horse out in the country as long as he didn't think too hard about the fact he could get shot.

Gideon reached the foothills in the late afternoon. He decided he had pushed Norse hard enough for the day and made camp when he came upon a creek with good grass surrounding the water. With nothing to do, Gideon dined on his hardtack and jerky and then crawled into his bedroll at dusk.

The early bedtime caused Gideon to awaken before dawn. By the time the sky began to lighten, he was saddled and ready to ride. As he ascended the foothills, he would slow the horse to a walk on the inclines and trot him down the descents. He occasionally spied tracks on the hard surface he hoped were made by Stanley's horse. The hills gradually got steeper and higher in altitude. Once he reached the top of a particularly tall rise, he pulled Norse to a stop to let the animal have a breather until they attempted the precipitous decline. Up ahead at the base of the hill, Gideon thought he spotted something brown in the roadway. He retrieved his spyglass from the saddlebag and studied the road below him. A brown horse lying on its side came into his view. The animal would occasionally move a leg or attempt to roll onto its chest before dropping back to the ground. While scanning the surrounding area, Gideon believed he spotted a whiff of smoke coming from behind an outcrop of rock. As he rested the horse, he plotted the locations where they could take cover if fired upon from below.

"All right, boy, let's see what happens." Gideon said.

He retrieved his Winchester from its scabbard and nudged the horse into a walk, hoping to make as little noise as possible. While he rode, he kept his eyes trained on the spot where he had seen the smoke. They were within a couple hundred feet of the downed horse when it raised its head and nickered at them. The head of a bearded man popped over the outcrop of rocks and then quickly disappeared again. Gideon, fearing he would get shot, steered Norse behind a rock shelf.

"Stanley, you need to surrender. Noel isn't dead. You won't be charged with murder," Gideon hollered.

"I've been in prison before and I ain't ever going back," Stanley yelled.

Gideon peeked above the rocks. Stanley waited with his gun ready. As Gideon ducked, the roar of the rifle echoed off the rocks. The bullet made a ricochet sound as it smacked the stone close to where his head had been.

"Damn it, Stanley. This doesn't have to end this way. You know I have to take you in."

"Only if I'm dead."

With his rifle ready, Gideon raised himself above the ledge. He and Stanley fired simultaneously. Neither shot found its mark but caused both men to retreat to cover. They continued taking potshots at each other with no success. Gideon grew weary of the game, fearing his luck could run out if this continued. He again popped up above the rocks and exchanged shots with the outlaw, but this time he did not retreat. After chambering another shell, he took aim on the spot he expected Stanley to appear and waited. Stanley darted his head up and Gideon squeezed the trigger. The force of the shot flung the prospector backwards, his hat and a spray of blood and tissue flying into the air.

Gideon took a deep breath and blew up his cheeks as he exhaled. He had no doubt the miner lay dead. After reloading his rifle, he rode down to the injured horse and dead man. The miner had a chunk blown out of his forehead and his eyes stared up into the heavens. Gideon retrieved the man's hat and covered his face with it. The horse had broken its leg from probably gaining too much speed coming down the incline. Gideon drew his revolver and put the old mare out of her misery. With no way to transport Stanley back to Last Stand, Gideon began the arduous task of covering the miner with rocks where the body had fallen.

"Sometimes I wonder why I stay in this job," Gideon said to no one and headed toward home.

Chapter 18

A couple of days after Finnie returned to work, he nearly felt back to being his old self. He still nursed sore ribs, and his black eyes made him look like a raccoon, but the dizziness had subsided. He and Gideon were drinking their first cups of coffee of the morning when Doc came in by himself.

"Where is Henry?" Gideon asked.

"He's staying with Noel right now. Noel has a bit of a temperature this morning. It's to be expected after the amputation. Overall, he's doing pretty well, but Henry feels responsible for him after treating him that first evening," Doc answered.

"He did a fine job that night. I don't know what we would have done without him," Gideon remarked for the sake of the doctor.

Doc grinned and nodded his head as he took a seat. "I tell you what, that boy is a natural. He has as fine of instincts when it comes to medicine as I've ever seen. He tied off that artery as if he'd been doing it for years. I couldn't have done it any better myself. He's going to make a fine doctor."

Finnie glanced over at the doctor. He was itching for some orneriness after days of not feeling well. "Maybe you should just up and retire and let Henry take over. His bedside manner is a big improvement over yours and he's certainly a lot quieter of a fellow than you ever thought about being."

The doctor slapped the arm of the chair. "I should have known you'd have something insulting to say. You are the most unappreciative man I've ever known. If not for me, that long Irish nose of yours would be going in about three different directions right now. Mary probably wouldn't even be able to ever look at you again. If Henry comes back here when he gets his degree, I just might retire so I can sit in here all day and keep you company."

"I don't know why I ever named my child after you. It's like naming him after the big bad wolf. You are nothing but an old codger," Finnie retorted, failing to conceal a grin.

Doc grinned, too. "Glad you're feeling better."

Gideon leaned back in his chair and ran his hand through his thatch of hair. "Now that you two have all your unpleasantries out of the way, can we move on? Doc, I think you need to take a look at Landon. He's not eating. He knows the judge will be coming soon and I think he is starting to feel the hangman's noose."

"I can look at him, but I can't make him eat."

"You do have a point there."

"What do you have planned for us today?" Finnie asked.

"If you feel well enough to ride, I figure we need to round up some more Indian boys. This has been dragging on long enough. Those damn miners are ruining this town."

Finnie quickly got to his feet. "I'm ready to get out of town anyway. I've been cooped up in that house for too long. Let's go for a ride."

"I guess I've stayed my welcome," Doc mused.

"You're like the john that when he got done with his business wanted to sit with the whore and have a nice little conversation. She told him she had as little time for him as his little man had to give to her," Finnie said and bobbed his head proudly for what he thought was a hilarious play on words.

Doc waved his hand through the air as if he were clearing smoke. Looking at Gideon, he said, "I'm glad you're riding with him and not me. I'm afraid I'd be tempted to just up and make him disappear out there somewhere."

"I doubt it would quiet him down any. We'd probably still hear him all the way back in Last Stand."

"You two are just jealous you aren't as witty as me. We Irish are known for our sense of humor," Finnie bragged.

Looking unamused, Doc shook his head. "You are known for something. That is for sure." He walked out of the jail before having to listen to Finnie's rebuttal.

Gideon headed to the cabinet and retrieved a couple of boxes of cartridges. "Go get your horse and rent a couple more from Blackie. We can put the boys on them."

"You really are serious about getting them all rounded up."

Closing his eyes, Gideon nodded his head. "I should have already had this done, but Charlotte's murder and all the shenanigans of these prospectors have kept us sidetracked. Those boys need us."

Finnie returned a short while later and the two rode out toward the river. Gideon planned first to find the boy he had spotted on the day he had tracked down the men responsible for Finnie's beating. They passed three prospectors working the river before coming upon the man with the Indian boy. When the prospector saw the lawmen riding his way, he put his arm around the boy's shoulders and pulled him against his leg.

Gideon pulled Norse to a stop and surveyed the situation. The miner looked defeated, his posture sagging and sadness in his eyes. The boy appeared fearful. In a voice void of malice, Gideon said, "We've come for the boy."

"Sheriff, I've never mistreated this boy once. I call him Rudy. I'm even teaching him how to talk English and everything," the miner replied.

"That may well be, but he was stolen from his home and you bought him. He has family that wants him back. You can't go around buying boys."

The miner pulled the boy tightly against his side. "But he's become like a son to me. I don't care a lick he's Indian. He's a fine boy. He can learn to live with white people and won't ever have to suffer on a reservation. Those people are treated like a herd of diseased cattle."

Gideon climbed down from his horse and walked toward the miner. "I appreciate your caring, I really do, but it still isn't right. It isn't your place or my place to decide what's best for Rudy. We are taking him with us. Please don't make this worse than it already is."

The prospector nodded his head slowly in defeat. He took the boy's head in his hands and looked into his eyes. "Go with Sheriff. He take care of you." He leaned down and kissed the boy on top of the head.

Gideon could feel melancholy sinking over him like a fog. Seeing the miner's despair over losing the boy had been about the last thing he had expected to witness that day. The encounter once again reminded him of his own grieving at the time of the death of his granddaughter. He held out his hand and the boy took it. The miner began to cry when Gideon lifted the boy onto one of the spare horses. As they rode away, the boy turned and waved to the prospector.

"Well, that was certainly surprising," Finnie said after they ridden out of the prospector's line of sight.

"I would say so. Kind of sad, really. That's the first of these miners that's showed up in Last Stand that I actually felt some compassion toward."

"The day is still young. I'm sure you'll feel differently about the next one."

Gideon let out a snort. "Probably so."

"Do you think we did the right thing? Maybe this boy would be better off growing up in our world. That man certainly cared for him."

"I don't know. From what I can tell, the Indians take good care of their children. I think they deserve to have their boy back."

"Probably so."

The lawmen headed upriver into an area they hadn't been to since the prospectors had started panning for gold. They followed the river for miles, passing several miners, but none with any Indian boys. Gideon had about come to the conclusion that there were no more boys in the area. He decided they would ride another mile or so, and if they didn't see anything, head for town. As they came around a bend in the river, they came upon a prospector and boy squatting on the bank while they panned. The man stood and faced the lawmen. He stood a little taller than Gideon and had the brawn to suggest he had spent time working in the bowels of a mine. His stance suggested defiance, and

WAYWARD BROTHER • 169

his eyes were narrowed to mere slits. The shirtless boy arose and stood behind the man.

"What do you want?" the miner asked in a loud and deep voice.

"We've come for the boy," Gideon replied in an emotionless tone.

"I bought him fair and square."

"The law says otherwise. We aren't looking for trouble. Just hand him over and we'll be done with you."

The miner glanced over at the rifle he had left leaning against a rock.

"I'll kill you before you ever lay hands on it," Gideon warned.

"Maybe you should just come and try to take the boy from me," the miner challenged.

Finnie drew his revolver from its holster and pulled the hammer back. "Maybe I should just shoot you on the spot," he threatened.

"Just about what I expected from lawmen. Never met one yet that didn't hide behind his badge," the miner spat out.

Gideon climbed down from Norse, and while keeping his distance from the miner, motioned for the boy to come to him. The boy made a wide berth around the prospector and walked up to Gideon. As Gideon put his hand on the boy's shoulder to guide him to the horse, he saw that the child's back was tattooed with welts and bruises. The blood began to throb in Gideon's temples. He clenched his mouth tightly shut and sucked in air through his nose. As he glanced up at the prospector, his eyes were filled with fury. He was so damn sick of all the mayhem the miners had brought to his little town. To his way of thinking, the sooner they were all gone, the better. Gideon let out a bellow that sounded like a cross between a Rebel yell and a bear's growl. The roar seemed strange even to his own ears and unattached from his body. The miner took a step back and appeared unnerved by it all. Gideon charged him. In his rage, he pummeled the prospector in a furious barrage of punches that forced the man to turn in an attempt to flee. Gideon clubbed the man in the back of the neck as he attempted to get away. The blow sent him sprawling face down into the dirt. With catlike reflexes, Gideon pounced onto the man, rolling him over and resuming the battering of his face.

"You are going to kill him," Finnie yelled as he pushed Gideon off the man's chest.

Gideon looked up at Finnie as if he'd just awakened from a dream. He glanced at the unconscious miner's bloodied face as his wits slowly came back to him. The beating he'd just administered gave him no feelings of remorse. He got to his feet and dragged the miner into the river, holding his head under water until he regained consciousness and began fighting for air. With a heave, Gideon flipped the man onto the bank and pressed a boot into his chest.

"If you are anywhere within twenty miles of here by morning, I will track you down and kill you like the vermin you are," Gideon yelled, applying more pressure with his boot as he did so.

"I'll be gone. I'll be gone," the miner yelled.

"You had better be."

Finnie walked over to the miner's rifle and picked it up. He worked its lever until all the cartridges were expelled then grasped the gun by the barrel and smashed it into the rock until it disintegrated. After tossing the Winchester aside, he lifted the boy on behind the first child and then mounted his own horse. He sat there waiting for Gideon to come, hoping he didn't have to drag him away.

Gideon resisted the urge to give the miner a good kick. He picked up his hat and adjusted it on his head until he had it just so before climbing up on his horse. "We might as well ride a little farther upriver. There are still two boys out here somewhere," he said as if nothing out of the ordinary had happened.

Finnie waited to speak until Gideon had his breath back. "With that fit you just threw, I think you might have even whipped me. I thought you were going to kill him," he said nonchalantly.

"You're probably right, I could have beaten you. I'm surprised I didn't have a stroke or have my heart explode. I shouldn't get that mad. It's probably not healthy, but I can't stand abusing a child. I don't know what makes people so mean. Everything he got, he had coming to him."

"That he did."

The two men rode on in silence while the two boys could be heard whispering in their native language. In the quiet, Finnie pondered what he had just witnessed. He'd seen Gideon's rage several times, but he wasn't sure if he had ever seen him as mad as he had been today. A part of Finnie felt proud of his friend, and another part worried for him. Sometimes he feared Gideon's sense of right and wrong was so strong as to be a burden that weighed him down. Finnie had never known another man with such a hypersensitive conscience. He still marveled that Gideon had spent fourteen years castigating himself in isolation for an accident. Glancing over at the sheriff, Finnie felt happy to call him a friend.

They found one more boy before the afternoon ended and retrieved him without an incident. After returning to Last Stand at dusk, they stopped to see Lloyd Peabody so that he could explain to the boys what would be happening to them. They decided Finnie would take the first boy, and Gideon would take the boy that had been beaten. With Pastor Roberts and his wife having had so much success with the child they had taken in, they decided they would watch the third boy.

As they were walking away from Lloyd's place, Finnie said, "I don't think we're going to find the last boy. Where else can we look? Do you think we should just give up and take these boys back to the reservation?"

Gideon rubbed his scar and sighed. "I've been thinking about that, too. I believe we need to make one more search and then decide, but these boys need to get home soon."

"You know, I just had an idea. We should have Lloyd explain to these boys that there is one boy missing and ask if they know where he is."

The plan seemed so obvious that Gideon couldn't believe he hadn't thought of it. He felt chagrined that Finnie had been the one to think of it. "That's a good idea. Maybe you are the brains of the operation."

"Of course, I'm the brains around here. I've always known why you dragged me to Last Stand. You get to have all the glory that way, and like usual, us poor Irishmen do all the real work."

Gideon grinned and shook his head. "Let's head back to see Lloyd. Then I need to stop in and get some salve for the boy's back from Doc. After that, I'm going home. This has been one long day."

"You might want to put some of that ointment on those bloody knuckles while you're at it."

Gideon held out his hands and looked at them in the fading light. He grinned sheepishly. "Quite a day."

Chapter 19

The interrogation of the Indian boys by Lloyd Peabody had led to the determination that the still missing child had been the first sold. From the description of the buyer, the lawmen figured he must have been a mountain man somewhere in the northwest part of the county. Gideon and Finnie had left the next day with a packhorse loaded with supplies for what the Irishman described as "Their pursuit of a needle in a haystack."

Abby had not been thrilled with Gideon leaving her alone with the Indian boy. The child did not appear to be a threat and had behaved himself, but she realized she would have her hands full if a problem did develop. Much to her relief, Winnie was fascinated with the dark-skinned child. The boy also seemed smitten by the older girl. The two of them, with Chance tagging along, spent most of their time outside playing or exploring nearby. The lack of a common language didn't prove a barrier to their adventures as they spent hours together. Winnie had taken to calling him Little Eagle and he had managed to learn the name of each member of the family. As Abby watched the children playing tag from the kitchen window, her trepidation began to wane. She just hoped Gideon would return soon. In her melancholy moments, she had begun to think of herself as the sheriff's widow.

At the Barlow homestead, Joann had been watching Zack work himself into total exhaustion every day since buying the Morris homestead. Using the pretext that she feared Elizabeth was developing a diaper rash,

Joann had convinced Zack to interrupt his clearing of brush to pay a visit to Abby for some advice. When their wagon pulled into Abby's yard, Joann did a double take at seeing the Indian boy chasing after Winnie.

"Either my family is being attacked by some mighty young Indians or Daddy found some more of those kidnapped Ute boys," Joann remarked.

"It has to be the latter. Winnie could whip a war party by herself," Zack joked.

"Be nice. That's my sister you're talking about."

"I meant that as a compliment."

"Sure you did," Joann said while passing Elizabeth off to her daddy.

Abby came bustling out onto the porch. "Is that my grandbaby you have there?" she playfully asked.

"We heard you were taking in strays," Joann quipped.

With a laugh, Abby said, "It would seem that way. Things are certainly interesting around here."

All the children followed the family into the cabin. With a deft maneuver, Winnie snatched Elizabeth away from Joann before Abby had the chance. She plopped down on the sofa and cradled the baby in her arms while Little Eagle and Chance joined her. The Indian boy was intrigued by the white baby and held out his finger for Elizabeth to grasp while Chance played peekaboo with her.

"That's something you don't see every day," Zack remarked.

"It's kind of sweet," Abby replied. She went on to explain all that had happened, and that Gideon had gone off looking for the last boy.

"Do you need us to stay with you?" Joann asked.

"No, I'm fine. He hasn't been any trouble. I'm surprised he's not leery of white people considering they stole him and beat him, but he seems to trust us."

The adults continued talking while the children attempted to amuse the baby. In midsentence, Abby abruptly stood and took Elizabeth away from Winnie.

"You had your turn and now it's mine. Take your brother and Little Eagle out to play," Abby ordered.

"But I haven't gotten to spend any time with Joann," Winnie whined.

"I'll be out shortly," Joann promised.

Winnie looked warily at her mother and sister but decided the time wasn't right for raising a ruckus. The last thing she wanted was for everybody to see her momma tear into her. She led the two boys out of the house.

Joann stood and turned toward Zack. "I left Elizabeth's diapers in the wagon. Would you go get them while I show Abs what I fear is going to be a rash? I know she needs changed anyway."

Zack nodded his head and walked outside.

Abby placed the baby on the sofa and began removing the diaper. "When did she start getting a rash?"

"She doesn't have one. I just used that as an excuse to get Zack over here, so you can talk to him. He won't listen to me, but I was hoping he would if it came from you. He thinks you hung the moon."

Abby looked up at her daughter, concern etched into her face. Zack and Joann's marriage was one thing in which she never troubled herself. "What's the problem?"

"Abs, ever since we bought the Morris homestead, Zack has about worked himself to death. We're making good money on him selling his alfalfa, but he thinks he has to have everything finished tomorrow. I wanted that land for our future. It's not as if we have to rely on it now. We just need to put some cattle on it and let it sit. He's going to find himself in an early grave if he doesn't slow down. You need to talk to him if you ever want another grandbaby. He's going to be too tired to ever make another one."

Abby let out a sigh, slightly relieved the news wasn't something worse than it was. "I think Gideon would have been better at this than me. Zack has a lot of respect for him and listens to what he says, but I'll do what you want. And for your information, I did hang the moon."

Zack walked back in with the bag of diapers. "How is the rash?" he asked.

Joann threw her hands in the air. "There isn't one. I just imagined things that aren't there. I'm going to take a walk with the children. Winnie wants me to spend some time with her. Abs needs you."

At that point, Zack began to get suspicious that something was amiss. Up to now, he had always accompanied them on their walks. He gave Joann a quizzical look but received back the most innocent looking expression imaginable from his wife. Now he knew for sure he'd been set up. Joann had never looked that innocuous since he had met her. He watched helplessly as Joann scurried out the door while Abby fetched a diaper from the bag and put it on the baby.

Dropping down onto the other end of the sofa, Zack said, "All right, Abby, I'm not the sharpest tool in the shed, but I'm smart enough to know when Joann is scheming. What is she wanting?"

Abby sat rocking Elizabeth in her arms. She turned the baby, so Zack could see his daughter's face. "You are right – Joann is guilty, but not of anything for herself for once. She's worried that little Elizabeth's daddy is going to work himself to death and not see this baby grow up. Joann says you are trying to get everything done all at once. I've got some news for you. There is always something on a ranch that needs doing. You're making good money – enjoy it and your family. None of it means a thing if you are too busy to have a life. Joann doesn't want to be a ranch widow – either figuratively or in actuality. She doesn't think you're listening to her, so she wanted me to give it a try."

Zack sat silently looking at Abby. He didn't know whether to be mad at his wife or thrilled she had gone to so much effort to try to get her point across to him. The clock's ticktock made the moments seem like minutes until he broke the silence. "But Abby, there is so much to do. I'm just trying to make a good life for us. That's all I want for Joann and Elizabeth."

"You already have a good life. On the day you die, there will still be things needing to be done. Nobody lying on their deathbed ever said they wished they had spent more time working. As long as you are providing for your family, be happy with what you have and work on the big plan a little at a time. God knows you had to work too hard to win the hand of that brat daughter of mine to grow apart because you are too busy. Zack, you know I love you just like you were my own. Promise me you'll slow down and enjoy your baby and wife. These babies don't stay this size for very long – believe me, they grow up fast. Be there to see it."

A grin came slowly to Zack's face and he could feel his cheeks get hot. Abby's show of feelings for him had embarrassed him. "I guess there are worse things in the world than having people care about me. I must be overdoing things if Joann is worried about somebody other than herself. I promise I'll slow down. Sorry to get you in the middle of this. Joann must be devastated that I'm not wrapped around her little finger tight enough any longer to get me to do whatever she wants," he said, trying to end things on a humorous note.

"Good, that's what I want to hear. That girl still needs to learn she doesn't always get her way though," Abby shook her head. "Such a brat."

"Everybody used to call her spirited back when I thought they were sugarcoating it. I'm the one that said she was a brat."

Abby laughed. "We called her spirited when she was single, and we were afraid nobody would have her. Now that she's married, we can call her a brat."

Joann slunk back into the cabin a while later. Her demeanor surprised Zack. He'd never seen his wife ever act reticent. She fidgeted with her hands as she looked at him. Zack couldn't believe his eyes. He snuck a wink at Abby before standing and towering over his wife.

"I can't believe you lied to me about a diaper rash just to get me over here so that you could get Abby to do your dirty work for you. I ought to put a rash on your ass," Zack threatened.

Joann's posture straightened, and she threw her head back. "Zackary Barlow, don't you dare talk to me that way. Daddy would shoot you dead if you ever laid a hand on me and you know it." Her voice sounded full of indignation.

Zack had to grimace to suppress a smile. Right before his eyes, Joann had transformed into the little banty rooster he'd come to expect and adore. "I doubt that. Gideon would probably cheer me on for finally giving you what you need."

"I was just worried about you, and you wouldn't listen to me. I thought you might listen to Abs. Excuse me for caring."

"Well, excusing you is one thing I'm used to doing. I did listen to Abby and I'm going to take her advice. It made sense to me. I have been working too hard."

In an exasperated tone, Joann asked, "Then why are you mad at me?"

"Oh, I'm not mad at all. I'm flattered that you care about me so much. I just wanted to see you squirm for once. It is a rare thing."

Joann pinned her hands onto her hips and stretched out her torso in an attempt to look taller. "That is just plain mean. I never knew you had a dark side . . ."

Abby arose quickly and thrust the sleeping baby into Joann's chest. "Take Elizabeth and don't you dare wake her. I would quit while I'm ahead if I were you. This is just a little payback for all the things you put this boy through back in your courting days. You are still way in the lead on such matters. You got what you wanted, so shush."

∞

Gideon and Finnie were on their third day away from home, weaving their way through hazardous mountain passes in search of the sixth Indian boy. They and their horses were weary from the exertions needed to negotiate the steep inclines. When they came to a mountain stream at a little past noon, Gideon pulled Norse to a stop to let the animals rest and to grab a bite to eat. He and Finnie sat on the bank and nibbled on jerky as the horses drank water and grazed on tall grass.

After Finnie tugged off a bite of the dried meat, he said, "Gideon, I want to find that boy just as badly as you do, but we haven't even come across another human being let alone the ones we're looking for. We have a better chance of getting struck by lightning."

Gideon stared at the rushing water passing by and didn't speak for a moment as he let Finnie's words sink in. "I know you're right, but damn you know how I hate to fail. Until I got out here in the middle of all this, I realized I had forgotten how big all of this is."

"That's true enough. The only way we're going to cross paths with that mountain man and the boy is going to be by sheer accident."

"One of those Indian families is never going to know what happened to their son. I can't imagine the pain." Gideon picked up a stone and skipped it across the water.

"We've gone to more trouble than most lawmen would do. I'd say there is only a handful that would have even bothered trying to find Indian children in the first place."

"I suspect you are right – not that that has a thing to do with us."

"Gideon, even you can't succeed every time. You just think you can."

A wry smile slowly came over Gideon. "So I've been told more than once."

"Just so you know, I'm willing to stay out here as long as you want. What are we going to do?"

With the skip of another rock, Gideon said, "Let's go home."

∞

A day of hard playing, along with the walk with Joann, had caused Chance and Little Eagle to fall asleep early without any prompting from Abby. She used the quiet time to teach Winnie how to hem a dress. They sat together on the sofa with two oil lamps on the coffee table to provide them with the light they needed for the delicate work of sewing. To Abby's surprise, Winnie was taking the instruction well without getting frustrated as she tried to master the craft.

Winnie set the dress down in her lap and looked over at Abby. "Momma, I'm sorry I'm always so difficult. I know I'm headstrong, and when I get my mind made up about something, I'm going to do it no matter what. I bet you wish I was one of those quiet girls that always behave."

The confession caught Abby so off guard that she hesitated a moment as she gathered her thoughts. She turned her body to face her daughter. "Gwendolyn Hanson, while it is true you can be difficult and are most certainly hardheaded and there are days where I would like to pinch your little head right off your shoulders, I wouldn't change a thing about you or want anybody else. Life can be hard, and you need determination to get through it without getting beat down. You'll be able to do that better than I ever dreamed of doing," Abby said. She took Winnie's head into her hands. "There are so many wonderful things about you, too. You don't lie or cheat at games. You are kind, and I couldn't ask for a better big sister for Chance. You are so good with him. You've always been a good little sister to Joann whenever she needed you, too, and you dote on Elizabeth. You love Gideon and he is crazy about you. If you had wanted to, you could have made things very unpleasant with him. You make me very proud. I thank God every night that you are my daughter."

"Really?"

"Yes, really. I bet, when you grow up, you'll be the best at whatever you decide to do. Whether you become a ranch wife like me or decide to become a lawyer or doctor or something else, you'll succeed. The world is changing for women and you'll make your mark."

"If I had the choice, I'd pick you for my momma, too."

"That's good to know, honey." Abby leaned over and kissed her daughter.

Chapter 20

Ethan arrived in Last Stand on his buckboard wagon and made his first stop at the feed store. Once the wagon was loaded with bags of oats, he guided the team of horses down to the general store to get some supplies. The mayor of Last Stand, Hiram Howard, greeted Ethan as he entered the store and enthusiastically helped him gather up the things on his list. Hiram was in his usual inquisitive mood and peppered Ethan with questions ranging from how his calves looked to how many members were attending his church these days. Ethan politely answered each inquiry as he hurried to finish his shopping.

With the supplies gathered, Ethan went up to the counter to pay for his purchases. "Hiram, I need you to order me a leather-bound journal with Benjamin's name embossed in gold lettering on the cover."

"What in darnation would Benjamin do with something like that?" Hiram asked, skepticism in his voice.

"What do you think? To write in, of course."

"That seems like pure folly for a boy to be wasting his time on. I'd think Benjamin would be more interested in hunting or Winnie Hanson than writing. Sounds like something a girl would do with a diary."

Ethan almost never got riled. It just wasn't in his nature to anger easily, but he found Hiram's tone to be a little condescending and thoughtless. He placed his hands on the counter and leaned over it slightly. "Benjamin thinks he wants to be a writer. I happen to believe that is a fine thing for a boy to dream of becoming. Not everybody has to follow in their daddy's footsteps. You never know, but he just might make Last Stand proud someday. If I recall correctly, most people believed it pure folly when you decided to run for mayor until you proved to them you were up to the task."

Hiram rubbed his chin as he met Ethan's glare head-on. "Ethan, I apologize. I didn't mean to offend you. I must admit I was being judgmental. If anybody could become a writer around here, it surely would be Benjamin. He's certainly a thoughtful boy and a model citizen. Again, I'm sorry. Please don't think ill of me."

"Apology accepted. I won't think of it again." Ethan leaned back and released the tension in his shoulders.

"I'll get that journal ordered for you and I'll give it to you at my cost to boot. When you offend Ethan Oakes, you know you've put your foot in your mouth." Hiram gave a nod and smiled.

Ethan grinned and returned the nod. After paying Hiram, he walked out carrying his purchases. He spotted Gideon and Finnie returning to town from their trek into the mountains. His two friends looked tired and defeated. Both men sported grim expressions and slumped shoulders. They merely nodded their heads in acknowledgment as they passed by the buckboard. Ethan hurriedly placed his packages into the back of the wagon and followed Gideon and Finnie to the jail. He managed to scramble down off the seat to walk with the lawmen into the sheriff's office.

"Where have you two been, and what went wrong?" Ethan asked as the men took their usual seats.

Gideon dropped his hat onto the desk and ran his hand through his hair before speaking. "We had one more Indian boy to find and we came up empty-handed. We've been up and down more mountain trails than I can count. We didn't see a soul let alone an Indian. I've failed on this one. We aren't going to find him."

"It surely isn't from the lack of trying," Finnie added.

"Oh, I understand. I'm sorry to hear that," Ethan replied as he adjusted his large frame to get more comfortable in the chair. "Gideon, you did your best. Nobody wins them all."

"So I've been told more than once lately."

"Well, it is the truth. You think you can right all the wrongs in the world and it just isn't possible. You do a remarkable job of keeping Last Stand safe, but some things are just out of your control."

"Good luck convincing him of that," Finnie complained.

After first scowling at Finnie, Gideon glanced over at Ethan. He didn't appreciate what they were inferring and wondered if they knew him at all. "Regardless of what you two may think, I don't hold some lofty vision of myself being a superior human being that can walk on water. God knows with my past that certainly is not the case, but I surely do hate to fail. I can't quit thinking about the family that will never see their boy again. Brings back some bad memories. That's the long and short of it."

Letting out a snort, Finnie said, "You might not think you walk on water, but you think you're superior to the average mortal."

Ethan reached over and touched Finnie's arm to get him to stop talking before turning his attention back to

Gideon. "That's commendable of you. Just don't be so hard on yourself. Nobody likes to see you get all down. You've had enough bad times to last a lifetime. Both of you look worn out and in need of some rest."

Gideon, deciding to ignore Finnie's remark, nodded his head, but didn't speak. He noticed a telegram on his desk and picked it up. After reading the note, he tossed it down without comment.

The gesture did not go unnoticed by Finnie. He stretched out his neck to get a look at the telegram. "What did it say?"

With a grunt and a rub of his scar, Gideon said, "It's from the marshal in Pagosa Springs. He thinks Fred is headed this way."

"That's what I figured. I knew you were sitting there too quiet after reading it. One way or the other, you are going to have to deal with Fred. You just aren't ready to admit it yet."

Gideon had heard about all he wanted out of Finnie. It seemed as if his friend was deliberately trying to rile him into real anger instead of his usual act of just trying to be annoying. Gideon slapped his desk and glared at his deputy. "I don't know what the hell is up with you today. I've never once said I won't deal with Fred if he becomes a problem. Granted, I may have said I didn't know what I would do if he showed up here, but we all know, when push came to shove, I would do what's right. As of now, we don't even know where he is or if the marshal is correct in his assumption. Fred knows I'm the sheriff in Last Stand. I don't know why for Heaven's sake he would come here when I've already help capture him once."

"Maybe because he knows you didn't have any choice the other time since you were with another sheriff. He might think things are different this time," Finnie shouted.

Ethan jumped up from his seat and positioned himself so he could get in between his two friends if they should come to blows. He had witnessed them irritate at each other too many times to count but had never seen them get to the point where he worried about a fight. "You two need to take a breath and calm yourselves. I've never seen you behave this way toward each other. You're both tired and frustrated. Finnie, you already look bad enough from the beating you took, and I have no doubt that Gideon would look even worse when you got done with him. Think of the friendships instead of the anger."

Gideon picked up his hat and slung it across the room in frustration. He decided it best to ignore Ethan's little dig about him coming out on the losing end of a fight. "I think Finnie must be jealous I might think more of Fred than him just because I have no desire to possibly have to kill a man that once saved my life. It is the silliest damn thing I've ever heard. Fred always was the third wheel in the group, but I take no pleasure in maybe having to bring him to justice. At one time, he was one of us – our brother."

The comments by Gideon seemed to take some of the starch out of Finnie. He slouched in his seat and held his tongue. An awkward silence followed until Finnie spoke. "I guess I have made too much out of this. Maybe I gave you a hard time because I didn't want to think about me having to take part in bringing Fred in either – I don't know. He was a darn good soldier and you could always count on him to have your back when things got nasty. Whatever Fred might have once been to us, the fact of the matter is he's now our wayward brother."

Ethan held out his hands. "Will you stand with me and pray?" he asked. Gideon and Finnie stood, and all grasped the others' hands. "Our Father in Heaven, I ask that you always keep the friendships in this room close to each of our hearts, so we always remember the love we have for each other that has been forged through years of trials and laughter. We ask that Fred Parsons be brought to justice without incident and by someone other than Gideon and Finnie. May you also bless Gideon, Finnie, and the Indian boys with a safe passage back to the reservation. And God, with the miracles that only you can bring into our lives, please let them find the sixth boy and return him to his family. Amen."

Gideon grinned first as he and Finnie eyed each other.

Finnie smiled and shook his head. "We better all quit holding hands before somebody comes in and thinks we're all sweet on each other."

As Gideon went to retrieve his hat, he said, "The day I get sweet on an Irishman is the day I have Doc make me a eunuch."

"They say that once you've been loved by an Irishman that nothing else will ever do," Finnie joked.

Ethan rolled his eyes. "Of course, they that said that were all Irishmen."

The three men broke into laughter.

"I wouldn't want to speculate on that," Finnie replied.

"I have to get home. You boys be good and have a safe trip if I don't see you before you leave," Ethan said and departed.

"What now?" Finnie asked.

"I say we get our supplies for the trip tomorrow and then leave Sunday on a buckboard with all the boys. I'm ready to get this over with."

"I dread this trip and I dread telling Mary. We're both liable to be served divorce papers by Billy Todd when we get back."

"Consider yourself lucky if that's all that happens to you. Abby is more likely to just up and shoot me. She can shoot a rifle better than most men."

"We do both have wives that are on the outspoken and lively side of life. Maybe we should have gone for those quiet and demure types," Finnie mused.

"Yeah, like either of us would be happy with that. We'd be bored out of our minds. Men like us need a wife that can challenge us."

The two of them chuckled at the thought.

Finnie put on his hat. "Let's go get something to eat and a beer. I'm about starved."

Chapter 21

The news that Gideon and Finnie would leave again so soon after their return from the mountains had put Abby in a melancholy mood. She refused to show how she truly felt about the situation though and made a point to be extra cheery to hide her feelings. And the truth of the matter was she felt happy the Indian boys would get to go home, but the thought of more time away from Gideon had her sneaking outside to have a good cry. She missed him terribly when he was gone. Back when Gideon had decided to become the sheriff, she had never in her wildest dreams believed he would be gone from home so often. With so many years having been wasted being apart, she didn't want to squander a single extra day.

Winnie, on the other hand, made no bones about her displeasure that her 'new little brother' was going home. When she heard the news, she started squalling and threw a temper tantrum before storming off to her room. Gideon gave her some time to calm down and then went to talk with her. It took all his resolve to hold his tongue as his precocious stepdaughter attempted to debate the subject with him. Only after he got Winnie to imagine her life if she had been kidnapped and forced to become part of a new family did he finally get her to accept that Little Eagle getting to go home was best for the boy.

On Sunday morning, Gideon rode to town with Little Eagle perched on the back of the saddle with him. When they reached the livery stable, Gideon left Norse there and rented a buckboard and a team of horses from Blackie. He also made the blacksmith the acting deputy, figuring Zack had enough on his plate. At the jail, Finnie waited with the other three boys. They all pitched in on loading the supplies onto the wagon. Once they finished the task, they rode out of town with the boys sitting on the supplies while excitedly chatting amongst themselves.

"How did Abby take the news of us leaving again?" Finnie asked.

Gideon let out a little snort. "She acted as if she was fine with it. In fact, she acted too fine with it. Makes me feel about six inches tall. Not that she intended it, but now I feel more guilty for being gone than if she'd thrown a fit. She was trying to be a good sport, but I know this is hard on her. Hell, it's hard on me. I hope this is our last trip for a while. Call me old, but I like waking up in my bed with my wife snuggled next to me."

Finnie had gone bug-eyed as Gideon talked. He tugged on the sheriff's sleeve for emphasis. "Mary did the same thing," he said excitedly. "At first, I thought she must be glad to get me out of her hair. Then I saw she had been crying. I pretended I didn't notice, but I realized what was going on. I really feel guilty for having believed she wanted rid of me for a while. We have us a couple of special girls – we really do. I'm going to get her something nice when we get back."

"That is a good idea. I'll have to put some thought in on what to get Abby. God knows they deserve something for putting up with us and the lives we've given them."

A bump in the road caused the men's shoulders to bounce together.

"This is going to be one long trip sitting on a piece of wood," Gideon grumbled.

"That it is. That it is."

The road going west out of Last Stand was in good condition and skirted the mountain ranges so that they made good time on their first day out. Only the occasional hill slowed their progress. In the afternoon, they came upon the South Fork Trading Post. The place sat near where the South Fork and Rio Grande rivers combined. Gideon and Finnie had only been inside the place one time when they were searching for a couple of killers. They had not been well received, and when the owner had pecked Gideon on the chest, the overprotective Finnie had badly beaten the much larger man.

"Maybe we should stop in and pay a social visit," Finnie joked.

"You're just in the mood to go thump on somebody to relieve your boredom," Gideon teased.

Little Eagle stood and excitedly tugged on Gideon's shoulder. As Gideon turned to see what the matter was, he pulled the team of horses to a stop. The boy pointed at himself and then at the other four boys. He then held up one finger before pointing at the trading post.

"I think he's trying to tell us the sixth boy is here," Gideon remarked.

"How could that be? They told Lloyd it was a mountain man."

"Actually, Lloyd used the term 'fur trader' and then described a longhaired dirty man. We interpreted that as a mountain man. All of it fits that sorry excuse for a human being who runs this place."

"Well, I'll be damned. All of that searching in the mountains for nothing when he was right here under our noses." Finnie shook his head.

"Maybe. I might have this all wrong, too." Gideon motioned for the boys to stay in the wagon. "Let's go have a look."

Gideon and Finnie walked into the dank, smoky trading post. The grimy place hadn't improved any since the last time they were there. As their eyes adjusted to the shadowy light, they spotted a couple of men drinking beer over at a table in the corner. The owner of the store looked up from behind the counter and took a step back in retreat at seeing the lawmen again.

"What do you two want?" the proprietor asked as he swiped his greasy hair out of his eyes.

"That's not a very friendly tone. We heard a rumor you have an Indian boy around here," Gideon said.

"I don't know anything about some Indian boy."

Gideon noticed the man's eyes dart to the side as he talked. The sheriff had been lied to enough in his job to recognize the sign when he saw it. "Where is he at?" he demanded.

"Sheriff, I don't know what you are talking about."

"I'm going to ask you one more time, and if you don't tell me, I'm going to unleash Finnie on you. You probably still remember what he did to you the last time you didn't mind your manners."

The man looked down at his feet, and in a quiet voice said, "He's out back."

"Finnie, keep an eye on him while I go have a look. I don't want you to lay a hand on him if he causes trouble."

"And why not?" Finnie asked in a perplexed tone.

"Because I want you to shoot him instead. We need to do our part to make this a better world."

Gideon maneuvered behind the counter and through a doorway into a room filled with junk of every sort imaginable before coming to the back door. Outside, he found the Indian boy attempting to split kindling with an ax that looked nearly as big as him. The boy dropped the tool and stood there looking as if he might make a run for it. Gideon knew enough sign language to make a quick gesture that he came in peace, and with the friendliest smile he could muster, he held out his hand for the boy. The boy looked around as if he were considering his options until deciding to take Gideon's hand. With a pat on the shoulder, Gideon led the boy back into the store.

"We have us all six boys," Gideon announced.

"I bought that boy. You're going to have to pay me for him."

"What is your name, by the way?"

"Bernard Sasser."

"Bernard, if I were you, I'd shut up and be glad we don't haul your ass off to jail."

"One of these days somebody is going to get tired of your ways and put a bullet in you," Bernard hollered.

Deciding it best they be on their way, Gideon let the threat pass. "Finnie, let's get out of here." He began leading the boy away.

"Hold it there a minute," Finnie protested. "Let's see what kind of jewelry he has. I'm sure Bernard is giving great deals today. As long as it's something nice, the girls don't have to know it's probably stolen."

Gideon let out a sigh and gave the Irishman a wary look but stopped walking.

Finnie moved to a glass case housing the jewelry. He began perusing the items and spotted a necklace that made his heart race and his knees go weak. Without bothering to ask Bernard to open the case, Finnie drew his revolver and smashed the butt into the glass, sending shards flying in every direction. He reached in and snatched up the necklace. When he flipped it over, he read, 'To Charlotte with love from Finnie and Mary.'

"Gideon, he has Charlotte's necklace."

"Where did you get that?" Gideon asked.

"I can't remember where I get all this stuff from. I have people trade with me every single day of the week. I don't even recall having that thing," Bernard protested.

Finnie glanced over at Gideon and received a single nod of the head. With a nimbleness that betrayed his squat appearance, Finnie pounced on Bernard and delivered a gut punch that doubled over his nemesis. As Bernard grabbed his stomach, Finnie sent a windmill punch into his jaw which sent the trading post owner flying onto his back. Finnie plopped onto the prone man's chest, pinning his arms.

"I'll give you one chance to tell the truth else I'll beat you to death," Finnie bellowed and landed another punch to drive home his point.

"Stop. Stop. I'll tell you everything. Fred Parsons brought that necklace in here about a month ago. He looked like he'd tangled with a bobcat. I took the necklace in on a trade for a revolver. I've done some business with him over the years. I haven't seen him since."

Finnie slowly lifted his weight off Bernard and stood. He fought off the urge to put a bullet into the useless excuse for a man before walking away, fearing he might change his mind.

Gideon had kept an eye on the other two men. They had done their best to act as if nothing was going on and continued to sip from their beers without looking over his way. "You two need to get out of here right now," he ordered.

The two men jumped up from their seats and headed for the door. Neither man said so much as a word.

Bernard managed to get to his feet, leaning his body onto the counter to stay standing. He supported his jaw with his hand as he worked it open and closed.

"Are we done here?" Finnie asked.

Gideon shook his head. "Bernard, we'll be back in about two weeks. When we return, I expect this place to be boarded up or in the hands of a new owner. If it is not, I swear to you I'll burn this damn place to the ground – that's a promise. You had better find honest work or I'm going to see to it that you rot away in my jail. Do I make myself clear?"

Bernard closed his eyes and nodded his head but didn't speak.

"Let's get out of here," Gideon said and lead the boy out the door.

The boys all stood and hollered a greeting upon seeing their missing friend coming out of the trading post. Gideon lifted the boy into the back of the wagon. The child began jabbering away excitedly at all he had just witnessed.

After the lawmen had climbed up onto the bench seat, Gideon asked, "Are you all right?"

Finnie opened his hand and gazed down at the necklace. "Not really," he said in a quiet voice. "One of my old friends killed a girl that was like a sister. It causes the memory of Charlotte's death to come rushing back to me and it makes me hate Fred."

"I know. And we've kept poor Landon locked up for something he didn't do. The only thing he's guilty of is taking a gun he won fair and square. I wish I had a way to send word to release him."

"Gideon, I'm going to kill Fred if I get the chance."

"I know you want to, but part of Ethan's prayer has already come true. I hope the part about somebody other than us bringing Fred to justice also comes to pass. We are the law and can't just gun him down. It would be better for both of us if he were arrested and hanged. I think either of us would be haunted by killing him."

Finnie turned toward Gideon. His eyes looked vacant and glazed. "Not me," he said.

Chapter 22

After Mary had purchased the Pearl West Saloon, she quickly came to the realization that converting it to a dance hall would require more work than she had originally anticipated. Her weekly Wednesday get-together with Abby and Sarah had fallen by the wayside because of the work. The other two women had also stopped meeting up once they got busy with gardens and other summer projects.

At church the previous Sunday, Abby had made it known in no uncertain terms that she expected Sarah and Mary to be at her home that Wednesday. She had discovered a huge raspberry patch while out checking the cattle and had plans for the women to go berry picking after their gab session. To ensure the plan came to fruition without distractions, she had even shipped Winnie and Chance off to stay with Joann the previous evening.

Mary arrived first with a batch of cookies she had baked that morning. Sarah showed up a few minutes later with a freshly baked apple pie. As the two women took seats at the table, Abby brought out her chocolate cake and a pot of coffee from the kitchen. She set them with the other desserts and joined them at the table.

Sarah snatched a cookie. "Oh my, I plan to founder myself on these sweets. I won't be able to eat for the rest of the week, but I don't care. I'm not about to start worrying about my figure today," she said and bit into the cookie.

"Me either," Abby said while cutting into the pie. She scooped out a slice and took her first bite. She closed her eyes as she savored the taste. "It used to bother me that everybody thinks you're a better cook, but not anymore, as long as I get to eat what you make, I don't care."

"Well, I am younger than you two, and if you both can keep your figures at your ages, I'm not worried about it either," Mary chimed in.

The two other women stopped in mid-bite, raising their eyebrows at Mary.

"Easy there, girl. The last thing us old broads want to be reminded of is the fact we're competing with a young thing like you," Sarah teased.

They all giggled before attacking the desserts.

"So, what's new?" Abby asked.

Sarah looked at Abby and then toward Mary as she debated whether to gossip. She decided the others could hear her news without getting a ruckus started between them. "Ethan told me he feared he was going to have to separate Gideon and Finnie in the jail the other day. He thought they were going to get into a fight."

"Really?" Abby said. "Gideon never mentioned it to me."

"Finnie didn't either. Those two are together too much. Sometimes they get on each other's nerves. And Finnie, God love him, doesn't know when to keep his mouth shut most times," Mary added.

Abby glanced over at Mary. She knew her friend was also one of Gideon's confidants, and that he might even talk to Mary about things he kept from her. For a brief instant, she felt jealousy. The moment quickly passed.

If there was one thing she remained confident in, it was that she was Gideon's only true love. "Did Ethan say what it was about?"

"It was over Fred Parsons. I guess Finnie rode Gideon about the fact they might have to deal with him, and Gideon got mad about it. Apparently, Gideon is torn up over his old friend now being an outlaw," Sarah replied.

"I told you it was Finnie's big mouth," Mary said. "He has it in his head that Gideon is going to look the other way and not do anything about Fred when the time comes. I told him to let it go. We all know Gideon will do right when it comes down to it. It's just his nature."

With a nod of her head, Sarah said, "That's something we can be sure of. We all probably know it better than Gideon does himself. His conscience won't allow for anything to not be right or at least his version of right."

Abby leaned back in her chair and looked at her friends. "It's a good thing I'm a secure person or I just might get jealous that you two know my husband as well as I do – maybe better."

Waving her hand through the air, Sarah dismissed the comment as nonsense. "While I won't argue that Gideon is a man that takes comfort in confiding in his women friends, you, my dear, are the apple of his eye. He sees the rest of us as just the tree to provide support. All of that is fine by me. I can truly say I love him like a brother."

Mary could feel her face getting warm and she didn't know what to say. Sarah's remarks had kind of put her on the spot. While she believed with all her heart that Finnie was the man of her dreams and that Gideon and Abby were destined for a lifetime together, she couldn't really call her and Gideon's relationship purely platonic. It certainly hadn't started that way, and even to this day, there remained a little spark between them that ran deeper than any friendship she'd ever known. "I just try to be a good friend to Gideon when he needs to talk," she blurted out.

Abby smiled at Mary, and reached over, embracing her friend's hand. She knew most women would fear the younger woman was a rival for Gideon's affections, especially since they had at one time been intimate, but she trusted both Gideon and Mary. While the occasional awkward moment did come up between the two women, Abby valued Mary's friendship and the counsel she provided to Gideon. "You are a good friend to Gideon. Both of you are. Let's stuff ourselves."

As the women continued to sample each other's desserts, Mary asked, "So how is the Benjamin and Winnie romance these days?"

With her mouth still filled with a bite of cake, Sarah said, "Don't ask me. Benjamin doesn't confide in me with that kind of thing anymore. I suspect he might still talk to Ethan, but I'll sure never hear about it."

"Winnie hasn't said anything to me lately either," Abby added. "The last time she mentioned anything, she said Benjamin acted shy around her these days and looked at her funny. I assume it must have been a lovelorn look."

"Oh, Lord," Sarah exclaimed, causing them all to burst into giggles.

"Wouldn't that be something if you two were tied together by marriage," Mary remarked.

"Sarah would hog the grandbabies," Abby chided.

"Yes, I would. You have two other children to give you grandbabies and you already have one now. Benjamin will be my only source of babies," Sarah complained. She paused and jerked her head up at the realization of what she had said. "That's not true. I have Sylvia now, too. For so many years, it was just the three of us that sometimes my mind still slips into that line of thought. And the idea of Sylvia someday having babies has never occurred to me until this moment. That sounded terrible."

"No, it didn't," Abby assured her. "It makes you sound normal and not so perfect."

Sarah chortled. "I'll be sure to tell Ethan that one."

A lull in the conversation followed until Mary looked up at the others with tears welling in her eyes. "Sometimes I miss Charlotte so much. It just comes over me like now when I'm with you girls. I guess it makes me aware of not talking with her."

Sarah reached across the table and patted Mary's hand. "I know you miss her. You and Finnie were so good to that girl. Time will lessen the blow."

"I wish I hadn't been the one to find her. That's something that will be seared into my mind forever."

"Once the trial is over and justice is served, maybe that will help," Abby added.

Mary shook her head. "I don't know that it will. I hate the way I feel toward that man, but I can't help it. I want him to suffer like Charlotte did. That's just not my nature."

"You are entitled to your anger. Just don't let it make you bitter," Sarah warned.

"I'm sorry I got sad. Let's talk about something else."

"Better yet, let's get to picking those raspberries or our butts might get too big to get out of these chairs," Abby announced while jumping up from her seat.

While Mary watched on, Abby and Sarah methodically hitched the team of horses to the buckboard. Buckets were loaded into the wagon along with Abby's rifle before the women climbed onto the seat and headed out toward the berry patch.

"Do you think you and Finnie will have any more children?" Sarah asked as they bounced along on the bumpy trail.

"I have no idea. I never thought I could have babies until the miscarriage. Sam still seems like a miracle to me. I try not to think about it and just let nature take its course," Mary replied.

"I always thought Ethan and I would have a large family, but it wasn't to be. That's why Sylvia has been such a blessing. I finally got my girl to raise. We all can't be as fertile as Abby."

"Maybe I just practiced more," Abby teased. She immediately turned red. Being audacious wasn't in her nature. Sarah was the one that had no qualms about speaking her mind about such things.

"Well, if practice is what did it, I think we can all agree that I'd be the one with a mess of children," Mary said, referring to her days as a prostitute.

Even Sarah didn't have a response to Mary's comment. An awkward silence ensued.

Mary ended the lull. "Ladies, we all know what I used to do for a living. You don't have to pretend you don't."

"You are right," Sarah chimed in. "And now you own half of Last Stand. Good in bed and good in business is a deadly combination."

The women broke into a fit of giggles. They rode on in a lively mood, teasing each other about their more noted personality traits and past transgressions until they arrived at the raspberry patch.

"They have thorns," Mary announced after climbing down from the wagon and inspecting the bushes.

"Well, of course they do," Sarah replied. "You are such a babe when it comes to some things."

"We didn't have raspberries in the orphanage," Mary protested.

"I suppose not. Just be careful and it's not too bad."

With the bushes loaded with berries from all the summer rains and warm weather, the women quickly began to fill their buckets. As Mary picked the fruit, she caught sight of a flicker of movement in the brush on an adjoining hillside. She studied the landscape but couldn't see anything until she spotted the motion again and recognized a tail. As she peered into the growth, she realized what she saw.

In a quiet voice, Mary announced, "There's a mountain lion on the side of the hill watching us." She pointed toward the cat with her finger.

Abby and Sarah gazed into the brush but couldn't spot the animal.

"Don't move," Abby ordered. She began slowly backing up toward the buckboard until she reached the wagon and retrieved the rifle. After chambering a shell, she shouldered the Winchester and pointed the gun in the direction where Mary pointed. "If that mountain lion charges, for God's sake, don't move. I'm liable to shoot you instead of it if you do."

The cat leaped from its hiding spot, traveling an amazing distance with each bound. Mary let out an ear-piercing scream but remained frozen in place as the mountain lion raced toward her. Without hesitating, Abby took aim and fired. As the gun roared, the cat winced and made an awkward step before resuming the charge. Abby quickly cocked the lever of the rifle and sighted again. The second shot felled the big cat a few feet from Mary. She screamed again and ran into Sarah's arms.

As Sarah hugged Mary and patted her back, she looked over at Abby. "Thank goodness you know how to use that thing."

"I've always said I could shoot and ride as well as any man," Abby boasted as she chambered another round and moved toward the cat to see if it were dead. "It won't be bothering us again. I hit it with both shots."

"We certainly will have a tale to tell about this adventure," Sarah noted.

"I can't believe that mountain lion charged us. They aren't known to bother people."

"He probably hadn't ever seen three pretty ladies just standing there for the taking. He had his eye on Mary though. I guess it pays for us old broads to keep a young one around to be the sacrificial lamb," Sarah said in hopes of bringing some levity to the situation.

Mary abruptly broke free of Sarah's embrace. "I have to pee," she called out as she ran into the brush.

Chapter 23

After five days on the road, and with one to go, Gideon, Finnie, and the Indian boys were bored and tired of each other's company. They had made good time with no delays, but the monotony of the travel had led to a couple of skirmishes amongst the boys that forced Finnie to crawl into the back to put a stop to before an all-out brawl ensued. Gideon and Finnie had run out of things to talk about and would go for hours with barely a word spoken between them. At times, Gideon found relief in the silence, and at other times, he contemplated starting an argument with the usually loquacious Irishmen just to relieve his boredom.

"Doc is going to be lost when Henry heads back to Boston," Gideon finally said to end the silence.

"I expect he will be. He'll be in the jail bothering us all the time just like he did before Henry arrived," Finnie mused.

"And arguing with you."

"He might like to fuss with me, but he likes to lecture you. He knows you're the one he has to keep on the straight and narrow."

Gideon shook his head in dismay. "Of course, I might have known you'd say something like that. Your halo just about blinds me."

"You know it's true. You are the one that gets all out of sorts and then thinks he can take on the whole world."

"And you're so perfect. As I recall you would have beaten poor Landon Noble to death if I hadn't stopped you, and he didn't even murder Charlotte after all."

"Sure, you can come up with one example for me. I've already thought about that and I feel terrible for acting that way. You are like the old whore whose eyesight was going bad. She looked in the mirror every morning and believed she was just as beautiful as in her youth. Just because you can't see it, it doesn't make it so."

"Where do you get all those whore sayings from anyway?"

"I just make them up off the top of my head. I've always been witty like that."

"I know they have certainly come to enrich my life," Gideon said sarcastically.

"I'd like to know how many hours of entertainment I've provided you since we first met all those years ago," Finnie said and pointed up ahead. "There's another wagon. Looks as if they have wheel trouble."

Gideon peered down the road and then glanced at Finnie and grinned. "I wonder what they'll think of us having a wagon load of little Indians."

The two men at the wagon stopped working and stood as the buckboard neared.

Finnie gave a wave to the men. "Hello, there. Maybe we can lend you a hand," he called out before they had come to a stop.

"We could use a little since we're not much good at this kind of thing. I appreciate the offer," one of the men called out.

At that point, the Indian boys all stood to get a view of what was happening. They began jabbering excitedly amongst themselves. Gideon looked over his shoulder to see what the matter was and saw them pointing at the men.

"Guns," Finnie yelled as he arose from the seat.

Gideon stood and had to flip the thong off the hammer of his Colt in order to draw his weapon. As he aimed the revolver, he heard Finnie fire his gun, followed by the roar of a return shot that made the unmistakable sound of smacking into the wagon. Gideon fired just as his target began to duck behind the wagon. The shot caught the man in the neck, sending out a cascade of blood. Finnie fired again and hit the other man. The shot didn't take the shooter down and he returned fire toward the wagon. Before the gunman could shoot again, Gideon and Finnie fired simultaneously, knocking the man to the ground.

"Disarm them while I check the boys," Gideon ordered.

Gideon set the brake on the wagon as Finnie jumped from the seat and ran toward the downed men. In the back of the buckboard, Little Eagle stood clutching his calf. The boy's fingers were covered in blood, and he looked as if he might pass out. Gideon laid Little Eagle down in the wagon and yanked the child's pant leg up above the calf.

"One of them is dead and the other soon will be. You must have severed his jugular vein. He's spewing out blood like a water pump," Finnie hollered.

"Get over here. Little Eagle is shot."

Gideon pulled a kerchief from his pocket and dabbed the blood away from the wound to get a better look. Once he knew what he was dealing with, he used the cloth to apply pressure to the injury.

"How bad is it?" Finnie asked as he jogged up to the wagon.

"It almost missed him, but it still took out a little chunk of meat."

Finnie began rummaging through the supplies. "I know we packed iodine and bandages in here somewhere that Doc sent with us. Let me find them."

Two of the boys jumped from the wagon and disappeared into the woods.

"Where do you think they are going?" Gideon asked.

"I don't have a clue. Found them."

Once Gideon finally got the bleeding to slow down, he doused the wound with the iodine. He was just beginning to wrap Little Eagle's calf with the bandages when the two boys returned with strips of moss. They held out the lichen as if they were presenting gifts.

"That's a good idea," Finnie said as he took the moss. "It sure worked in the war."

Finnie held the moss against the boy's leg as Gideon wrapped the bandage around the wound and taped it down.

"I think he'll be fine as long as we keep that wound clean," Gideon said as he pulled the boy's pant leg back down.

Little Eagle sat up and braced himself with his arms. He still looked a little glassy-eyed, but his color was returning. Gideon tousled the boy's hair, prompting a smile. Not to be outdone, Finnie signed to the boy that he was now a warrior. He got a nod of the head in agreement.

"I guess we found our kidnappers. I sure wasn't expecting that to happen. From now on, maybe we should assume everybody is an outlaw and have our guns ready," Finnie remarked.

"That and don't get distracted by chatty Irishmen."

Finnie narrowed his eyes and shook his head. "You would have been shot while looking backward if not for me. We Irishmen might be a wee bit talkative, but at least we're not ungrateful like you Germans. What are we going to do with the bodies?"

"We are going to drag them into the woods and leave them. I want to get these boys home and not waste time. It serves them right anyway for stealing these boys. Let the wolves have them. We'll tie their horses behind the wagon and give them to the tribe. I'm sure they could use them."

With a nod of his head, Finnie jumped from the wagon and began walking toward the other team of horses. "I guess we found out what these men thought about our little Indians."

"Hey, Finnie, I hope you realize that I don't know what I'd do without you. I'd probably give up this job."

"Write that down and sign it. I'm sure I'll need to show it to you by tomorrow at the latest."

Once the horses were tied behind the wagon and the bodies moved, the journey resumed. Gideon pushed on until darkness had nearly descended over the land before making camp. By that time, Little Eagle was in a good deal of pain. Nonetheless, the boy limped off to help gather firewood. Finnie, fearing the boy would reopen the wound, sat him down and showed him how to open cans of beans to keep him occupied. After the fire was burning good, Finnie fried some salt pork and warmed the beans. Everyone was hungry from not eating since breakfast, and quickly devoured the food.

As Finnie cleaned the plates, Gideon got the boys to bed. The men were tired from the long day and crawled into their bedrolls a short time later.

The following morning, the boys were served a cold breakfast as Gideon was in no mood to dally. Little Eagle had slept poorly, and his face showed the strains of his ordeal, but the wound looked good. Before heading out, Gideon treated the injury with iodine and applied fresh moss along with a clean bandage.

Late in the afternoon, they finally reached the reservation. Word of their arrival spread like wildfire, and they were soon surrounded by what looked to be the whole tribe. The crowd began shouting out in celebration as parents ran up to the wagon to find their children. In all the commotion, Cany managed to climb onto the wagon and greet Gideon and Finnie.

Simon, the Indian that had spoken to them in English on their previous visit worked his way up to the wagon. "You are men of your word," he called out above the noise.

"We try," Finnie shouted. "We also took care of the two responsible for stealing the boys. You won't have to worry about them again."

"Good. We will celebrate tonight in your honor."

Gideon and Finnie were led off into a teepee where they sat with a group of Indian men and shared in the smoking of a ceremonial pipe. After the ritual was completed, they were served a stew.

"This sure is tasty. I wonder what's in it," Gideon mused.

"I wouldn't want to speculate on that," Finnie replied. "These Indians are fond of things that might not sound so appealing to us."

Simon listened to the men's conversation. He smiled knowingly but made no comment.

As nighttime fell, the men were seated at a roaring fire while the celebration began. For the next three hours, they were entertained by dancing, singing, and drumming. At the end of the performances, Simon presented both men with a single-strand, bird-bone necklace with an attached piece of turquoise mounted in silver.

Simon placed the necklace on each man. "We thank you for returning our young men. You will always have a place in our hearts. Wear this necklace as a sign of your friendship with the Ute Nation."

Afterward, the men were led to their sleeping quarters.

"Maybe they'll present each of us with a woman for the night," Finnie joked.

"It would be the last woman you ever had if Mary found out. She'd cut your pecker off while you slept and throw it out in the street for the whole world to see."

"Aye, I was only joking, but you have summed up the situation succinctly. That woman is not to be trifled with. I can't wait to get home to her."

Chapter 24

Gideon and Finnie had pushed the team of horses as hard as they dared to get home as quickly as possible. Further aiding their speed of travel was that the return trip had gone without any incidents to slow them down. With the reduced weight from the dwindling supplies and not having the boys along, they had managed to shave a day off their travel time. As they passed the South Fork Trading Post, the lawmen had been amused to find the place locked up and Bernard Sasser nowhere in sight.

"Do you think somebody else will take over the trading post?" Finnie asked to break the monotony.

"I think Bernard will open it back up as soon as he's sure we've passed by. He knows we almost never come this way. I suspect you'll get to terrorize poor Bernard once again one of these days."

"He surely does leave a bad taste in my mouth." Finnie spat as if just the memory proved enough to leave a vile aftertaste lingering on his tongue.

"We should be home by sunset. I can hear my bed calling me now."

"The bed and the woman in it. Mary, honey, you don't need to wear flannel tonight – I'll keep you warm."

Gideon shook his head as they both cackled.

The men continued their eastward trek for the rest of the afternoon, and with the sun setting at their backs, they rode into Last Stand. Gideon immediately noticed that there were an awful lot of people milling about on the street for a Tuesday evening. Mayor Howard came running toward the wagon with his arms flapping like a loon trying to take flight.

"Thank God you two are back. I just got robbed about an hour ago. I thought he was going to kill me," the mayor shouted.

Gideon pulled the wagon to a stop and let out a huge breath. The exuberance he'd felt moments before upon seeing his town was already gone, replaced with a sinking feeling for what he was about to hear. He rubbed his scar. "Tell me everything."

"Like I said, about an hour ago this man came into the general store wearing a mask. He took all my money and fired his gun over my head. About scared me to death. That's the first time I've ever been shot. He rode off going south out of town."

"Blackie didn't go after him, did he?"

"No, he wanted to, but I wouldn't let him. I don't want a blacksmith getting killed over my money to be on my conscience."

"That's good. What did you notice about the gunman's appearance?"

"He was left-handed. I noticed that. He looked thin and on the small side with dark hair. Oh, and he sounded like he talked through his nose. That's about all I could tell you."

Gideon glanced over at Finnie, wondering what the Irishman's reaction would be. Finnie looked troubled by the news, shaking his head in disbelief.

Blackie jogged up beside the wagon. "Gideon, I wanted to go after him, honest, but the mayor wouldn't let me."

"That's fine, Blackie. I made you the deputy to watch over the town, not to chase robbers. There's nothing you could have done to stop this. I'll chase the outlaws and you keep my horse well shod."

"What are you going to do?" Mayor Howard demanded.

"Damn, Hiram, what do you think we are going to do? We'll find him, but it's not going to be today. Get back to your store and let me deal with this," Gideon said. He tapped the reins on the horses' rumps to leave before he said something he would regret.

Finnie didn't say a word until they walked into the jail. "What now?"

Gideon retrieved the cell keys from the top of his desk and tossed them at Finnie. "First off, let's free an innocent man."

With a snatch of the keys out of the air, Finnie disappeared into the cell room. He returned moments later with Landon following him. The young prospector glanced about the room warily as if expecting something bad to happen. He nervously rubbed his gaunt face with his bony fingers as he worked up the nerve to look the sheriff in the eye.

Gideon held out his hand to shake. "Landon, we now know you didn't kill Charlotte. I sincerely apologize for the time you've spent locked up. I hope you can find it in your heart to forgive me."

Landon set his jaw and looked as if he might speak his mind until thinking better of it. He hesitated a moment and then shook hands with the sheriff. "Apology accepted."

"Glad to hear it. Let me get your rifle," Gideon said. He retrieved the gun from the rack and grabbed a new box of shells from the shelf. After handing them over, Gideon fished a twenty-dollar gold piece from his pocket. "I hope this tides you over until you get back on your feet."

"Thank you, Sheriff."

"It's the least I can do."

As Landon reached the door to leave, he turned back toward the lawmen. "How do you know I won't go outside and load this rifle and come back in here and shoot you?"

Gideon smiled knowingly. "Because anybody that feared hanging as much as you do, sure wouldn't put himself right back in the same situation."

Landon grinned. "That's a good point. Though I might be tempted to go in there and plug Alvin in his cell. He's the one that started this whole mess."

"You're young. Go out and make something of yourself."

The prospector nodded his head and walked out of the jail.

When the door closed, Gideon dropped into his chair so forcefully that the padded leather sounded as if it groaned. "So much for welcome home," he muttered.

"You can say that again," Finnie said and took his seat.

"Why in hell come here to rob? He has to know I'll come after him."

"I don't know. Maybe he's taunting you or maybe he's tired of running and wants to get caught."

"Fred doesn't strike me as the type to want to go back to prison, especially since he'll more than likely hang now instead. I just don't understand."

"Gideon, it really doesn't matter why. It just is what it is."

Gideon leaned back into his chair. He gulped a breath of air, rubbed his scar, and blew up his cheeks as he exhaled. "I'm really going to have to deal with him, but we are doing this my way. I intend to bring him in alive."

With a nod of his head, Finnie said, "Just as long as I'm the one that gets to put the noose around his neck."

"Doesn't it bother you even a little to have to bring in somebody that fought with us day in and day out for years?"

"He didn't have to kill Charlotte. Now he's nothing more than a cold-blooded murderer. You and I both know if we don't get him, he'll kill some other innocent person – just like a dog that gets a taste of chicken blood. Next time could even be somebody more dear to us than Charlotte. No, sir, Fred destroyed what would have been a lifetime of loyalty."

As Gideon leaned forward, he clicked his fingernails a couple of times on the wooden desktop as he decided what to do. "Let's go home and then get on this first thing in the morning."

Gideon returned the wagon to the livery stable and retrieved Norse. He let the horse set his own pace home, loping most of the way in the light of a nearly full moon. On the ride, Gideon tried not to think about tomorrow or anything else except for getting home. When he reached the cabin and rode into the yard, Red started barking and clued the family to an arrival.

"It's just me," Gideon bellowed.

"That's a good way to get shot," Abby announced.

"Looks like everybody did just fine without me," Gideon said as he climbed down from Norse and was mobbed by his family.

"Momma had to shoot a mountain lion," Winnie blurted out.

Abby gave Winnie a stern look before turning her gaze to Gideon. "We can talk about that later. How was your trip?"

"Long. Let's get inside. I haven't eaten. Do you think you can fix me something?"

"I just think I might."

Once inside, Winnie noticed the necklace hanging out of Gideon's shirt. "Where did you get that?" she asked with wonder in her voice as she reached up and touched it.

Gideon put his hand to the necklace and rubbed the turquoise. "The Ute tribe gave Finnie and me each one of these for returning Little Eagle and the other boys." He removed the necklace. "I want you to take it for safekeeping for me."

"Really?" Winnie asked as Gideon placed the necklace over her head.

"Sure. A pretty necklace needs to be worn by a pretty girl."

Winnie fingered the bird bone a moment before running to the stove to show Abby her new jewelry.

"That is beautiful, Winnie. You'll have to take care of it. It isn't a toy," Abby warned.

"I know, Momma. I'm not a child."

While Abby fried eggs and bacon, Gideon told of the trip, leaving out the part of Little Eagle getting shot. Winnie made sure she was next to recount all that had gone on in her life while Gideon was gone. Chance remained content to sit next to his father at the table and listen. He made sure their chairs were touching so he could lean against Gideon.

"So, tell me about this mountain lion," Gideon said after Winnie had finally stopped talking.

As Abby brought the food to the table, she quickly recounted the events of that day, trying to sound as nonchalant as possible.

"You girls need to be more careful," Gideon chided.

Abby put her hands on her hips and peered at her husband. "It wasn't like we were standing around saying 'Here kitty, kitty, come get us.' I've only heard of a time or two of a mountain lion attacking people. He probably thought Mary was a doe with her big dark eyes."

Gideon grinned but didn't take the bait on commenting on Mary's appearance. "I'm just glad you're a good shot – good as any man," he said to flatter Abby.

"That sounds better."

The family sat around the table for another hour talking before Abby sent the children to bed. They kissed Gideon goodnight and Abby went to tuck them in.

When Abby returned, she took a seat across the table from Gideon. "What are you not telling?"

Gideon got up from his seat and retrieved his pipe and tobacco. He carefully packed the tobacco and lit it. Women still amazed him. Sometimes he felt as if he must have a sign on his forehead. "Fred robbed the general store today. And we found out that he killed Charlotte. Finnie and I are going after him tomorrow."

"That evil man. He's an animal. I'm truly sorry for you and Finnie. I know how you've been dreading this for a while now."

"Comes with the job, I guess. I'm sorry I have to be gone again."

"And that comes with the job, too, though I am starting to feel like a sheriff's widow. When this is all settled, we're sending the kids to stay with Joann for a couple of days and have us some alone time."

"You won't get any argument from me. Abby, what if I have to kill Fred?"

"Gideon, you'll just be doing your job. You are sworn to uphold the law. Fred has forfeited any loyalty you owed him, and he knows it."

"I suppose you have a point, but we all know I bend the rules sometimes."

"Letting Fred go would be breaking, not bending the rules."

"I know."

Abby reached out and ran her finger down Gideon's nose. "Of course, you do. I'm going to heat you some water, so you can take a bath and then get you to bed. You need one night's rest before you go back on the road."

"Earlier today, I planned on getting a little loving tonight. I think the mood has about left me now."

With a wink, Abby stood. "That's all right. I've been running a tab for you. You have quite the debt you owe me when you get back."

"Well, I am a man that believes in paying his debts."

When Gideon finished his bath, he felt so relaxed that he could barely keep his eyes open. Abby led him to bed and he was snoring by the time she changed into her nightgown.

Gideon awoke at the crack of dawn and tried to get out of bed without waking Abby but failed in his attempt. His plan for a quick departure was thwarted when she insisted on fixing him a proper breakfast before he could leave. As Abby lit the kindling and began preparing the food, Gideon bided his time checking his guns.

When the food was cooked, Abby brought the bacon, eggs, biscuits, and gravy to the table, and began filling both of their plates.

"You're going to get me fat," Gideon remarked.

"You always lose weight on your trips. You look too thin. If it weren't for me, you'd shrivel up to nothing."

"Well, we wouldn't want that."

"Gideon, promise me you won't do anything foolish just because Fred used to be like a brother to you."

"I'll be careful, but I plan to take him alive."

Abby paused in forking a bite of egg toward her mouth and studied her husband. She knew he had skirted the promise and that there was no point in pushing him any further. "Just remember you have a family that needs you."

With a smile and a nod of the head, Gideon tore off a chunk of bacon.

After the breakfast was eaten, Gideon kissed Abby and then made a hasty departure. He arrived at the jail just as the sun broke the horizon and found Finnie waiting for him.

"I didn't get a packhorse. You didn't say anything about it. I figured we were traveling light," Finnie said.

"Yeah, I hope we make short work of this. Let's get this over with."

The two men mounted up and took the road south out of town. The first few miles had too many tracks to try to figure out which ones belonged to Fred, but they didn't find any that had left the roadway, and eventually, the hoofprints thinned down to a single set of tracks.

"I hope we didn't miss something. I'd hate to track these hoofprints all day and it leads to nothing," Finnie worried.

"I think we're on the right trail. I've noticed this set of tracks for a while. The rider has been pushing his horse pretty good."

"Don't you find it odd that Fred robbed Hiram in broad daylight? We would have been hot on his tail if we'd been there."

"I thought about that, too. My guess is he knew we weren't there. Maybe he did some checking around town, or my bet is he had a conversation with our friend Bernard Sasser."

"That sounds about right. We need to throw Bernard in jail the next time he crosses us."

A little farther down the road, they found the still warm embers of a campfire.

The lawmen rode all day, deeper into the mountain ranges. For the most part, the trail followed a creek that made travel relatively easy and provided occasional glimpses of the horse tracks.

"Where in the hell do you think Fred is going? This leads to nowhere as far as I know," Finnie muttered.

"No idea. I've been expecting the tracks would turn east through one of these mountain passes. Maybe he knows of a hideout down here somewhere."

"How far ahead of us do you think he is?"

"I don't think Fred is very far away at all. From the looks of his tracks, he hasn't pushed his horse since he made camp last night. I don't think he believes anybody will be coming for him."

As darkness descended, Gideon was about ready to stop for the night when a light appeared up ahead. They sat on their horses and watched as a campfire took hold and began blazing.

Gideon let out a loud sigh. "I guess this is it. We can walk in from here."

"I hope we can find some cover when we get there. We can spread out and have him covered," Finnie suggested.

"No, I'm walking into his camp. I think that's the best chance of taking him alive. Otherwise, he's liable to try to fight it out."

"You're liable to get yourself killed, too. I'll be the one that has to tell Abby that her knuckleheaded husband is dead."

"I can't help it. I just don't want us to be the ones that kill Fred."

"Well, I'm going in with you. Don't you dare try to stop me. You are not the only one that can be bullheaded."

Gideon glanced over at Finnie and decided there was no point in trying to change his mind. "Let's go then."

They proceeded along the edge of the creek until they were standing in the shadows of the campfire. Fred was hunched over the fire, oblivious to his surroundings as salt pork sizzled in the skillet. Gideon gave a nod of his head and the two men stepped into the light. The snap of a stick underfoot caused Fred to look up. He stood slowly as he recognized Gideon and Finnie.

"I heard tell you boys were off playing with the Indians," Fred said jovially.

"We got back in town yesterday," Gideon said.

"That was bad timing on my part then. I was under the impression I had a few more days. Look at you, Finnie, all cleaned up. The last time I saw you, you were sleeping in horseshit."

"Gideon got me off the bottle."

"Good ole, Gideon. I always thought he'd make a good mother. At least until he killed that boy."

Gideon dropped his hand to be near his revolver. "Fred, we are taking you back to Last Stand. Charlotte, the girl you murdered, was a friend of ours."

The mention of Charlotte brought a pained expression to the outlaw. "I never aimed to kill her. I really believed she had gone for the night. She came at me like a bobcat protecting her kittens."

"You could have just got out of there. She was like a sister to my wife and me," Finnie said.

"That little hellcat would have chased me into the street and hollered until the whole town came running. She didn't give me much of a choice, but it pained me, nonetheless. So, you're married. That's even harder to imagine than you being a deputy. My, the times do change."

Gideon took a step to the side so that he and Finnie were not shoulder to shoulder. "Yes, they do. I never would have ever guessed you'd become an outlaw or intentionally kill an innocent girl."

"I guess we'll both have to answer for killing young ones someday – maybe today. I'm not going back just to be hanged or to spend another day in jail. If you want me, you'll have to kill me," Fred said as he pulled his jacket behind his holster. "Boys, back in the day, it was an honor to call you my brothers."

"You, too, Fred," Gideon said. "It doesn't have to end this way."

Fred went for his gun. He rushed the draw and fumbled getting a clean grip of the revolver. Gideon and Finnie fired their Colts a tick apart. The shots tore into Fred's chest, sending him stumbling backward and collapsing. Finnie dashed over to Fred while Gideon stood frozen in place, staring down at his gun.

"He's gone. Looks like one of us got him in the heart," Finnie called out in a quiet voice.

Gideon holstered his gun and slipped the thong over the hammer. "You were right all along. We were going to have to deal with Fred before all was said and done."

"You gave him his chance. You can't blame yourself."

"I know I did, but sometimes I hate this job. Think of the irony in that I wouldn't be standing over the dead body of Fred Parsons right now if he hadn't saved my life all those years ago. Sometimes I think our whole lives are determined by the whim of which direction the wind blows." Gideon retrieved Fred's blanket and covered the body. "In the morning, we'll take him home. We at least have reward money coming. I guess that's something."

"I'll grant you that luck and chance play a large part in where our lives lead, but our hearts point us in the direction we choose."

"Well said, my friend."

Chapter 25

With Henry set to leave to return to Boston on Monday, Mary decided to throw a little going-away party for him on Sunday night at the Last Chance. All Doc's friends and their families were there. Mary had even hired some musicians and they were playing an Irish jig that had Finnie showing off his dancing skills. The rest of the men stood around the two tables covered in food brought over from the café. They laughed at him as they sampled the snacks. Gideon had brought a box of cigars and they were all puffing on them and smoking up the place. The women sat at a table, drinking beer, and talking.

"This beer is an acquired taste," Abby remarked. "The more I drink it, the more I want to acquire it."

The other women broke into a fit of giggles as if Abby had just said something hilarious.

Abby twisted her torso to shield Elizabeth from some of the noise. "You hens are going to wake the baby."

"Abs, she's a sound sleeper," Joann reminded her mother.

The band launched into "Cupid's Chase Waltz." Mary watched as Winnie taught Benjamin the steps. Winnie laughed and smiled the whole time while Benjamin looked as solemn as a preacher as he tried to master the dance. "Those two have no idea how lucky they are to come from such fine families," Mary said with a touch of envy. "Of course, they shouldn't have any idea. No child should know any differently. They are so cute together."

"I'd take Benjamin into the family in a heartbeat," Abby announced. "I couldn't do any better than that boy and Zack. I don't think it's a fair trade though. My daughters seem to be too free-spirited for their own good."

"Abs, you wouldn't change a thing about Winnie and me even if you could and you know it," Joann bragged.

Abby grinned at her daughter but didn't reply.

Sarah was dying to hold the baby and she snatched Elizabeth from Abby's arms without asking. "Time will tell if those two remain fascinated with each other, but Benjamin needs a girl such as Winnie. He's like his daddy. They get set in their ways if you don't shake them up once in a while and keep them on their toes."

"I think that's true of all men. It certainly is for Finnie," Mary mused.

"Maybe so," Sarah conceded. "But I still think it is more so with the ones like Ethan and Benjamin. They can get so serious about everything. At least Finnie finds humor in all the craziness in the world."

Abby nodded her head toward the other children. "Sylvia is so good with Chance and Sam." The youngsters were singing and playing a game of "Ring Around the Rosie."

"That's another headstrong little female," Sarah noted. "But she's a keeper."

Joann, in her slightly inebriated state, pointed at Blackie. "You old broads should find Blackie a woman. He's a sweet man."

"I hope you weren't referring to me," Mary said.

"No, of course not. I meant Abs and Sarah. You're still young, like me."

"Abby and I are young enough that we could still have babies. We are not old, but we are wise enough to know how to handle an impertinent thing like you. I can still tan a butt if I have to," Sarah boasted. "But you are right. We just might have to find Blackie a mate."

"What about Delta?" Abby asked.

Delta was scurrying around the saloon keeping drinks filled.

"You know, that's not a bad idea," Mary said. "She certainly deserves a good man."

Zack walked over to the women and went to retrieve Elizabeth from Sarah.

Sarah held up her hand to thwart the young father. "You get out of here with that nasty smelling cigar. Your baby doesn't need to breathe that foul air."

"You're right," Zack said. He made a hasty retreat back to the other men, causing the women to break out into another fit of giggles.

Gideon was talking with Henry. He promised the young man that next summer Finnie and he would make the time to teach him how to shoot and box. Ethan walked up to them and tugged on Gideon's sleeve to get him away from the noise.

"What's going on?" Gideon asked after they moved to a corner.

"I just wanted to check on you and see how you were doing. Today at church, I didn't get the chance to be alone with you. I know killing Fred had to be hard on you," Ethan said.

"I've made my peace with the whole thing. Believe me when I say I've learned my lesson about carrying around guilt. It sure wasn't what I wanted, but Fred didn't give us any choice. Sometimes I wonder if we ever really know another person."

"Probably not. I think some people just get tired of trying to make an honest living. Maybe they are a little lazy, too. A life of crime seems easier than hard work. Could be that's what happened to Fred. It still doesn't take away that there was a time when he was a good friend to you."

"I think you're right about Fred. And I'm going to be fine. I've come too far to go back to the dark days. These are the good days."

The band took a break and Doc used the lull to get everyone's attention. He pulled Henry to his side and put his arm around the young man.

"I want to thank Mary for having this wonderful party for Henry. She has been a special friend to me for a long time. Henry and I both appreciate the gesture. Sometimes I wonder what I ever did to receive so many blessings in my life. I'm so proud of my grandson. He's already proved he is going to be an excellent surgeon by saving Noel's life. Who knows, but maybe he will take my place here in Last Stand someday. I'm sure going to miss Henry when he leaves, but I know I'll have all of you to look out for me and keep me company, or in Finnie's case, keep me riled up," Doc said and then paused as everyone laughed. "Getting to know my son and his family back east these last few years has been the greatest gift I've ever received in my life, but the kindest thing I've ever experienced is that all of you made me a part of your families many years ago. I'd like everybody to join me in a toast – to family."

About the Author

Duane Boehm is a musician, songwriter, and author. He lives on a mini-farm with his wife and an assortment of dogs. Having written short stories throughout his lifetime, he shared them with friends and with their encouragement began his journey as a novelist. Please feel free to email him at boehmduane@gmail.com or like his Facebook Page www.facebook.com/DuaneBoehmAuthor.

Made in the USA
Columbia, SC
11 April 2021